A CATTLE RAISER
AND HIS PROBLEMS

"Hatchet came from Texas—the Panhandle, south of Iubbock—about thirty-five years ago, trailin' in its base stock."

"Why did it leave Texas?"

Will hesitated, then said, "Farmers drove it out. Windmilla an' barbwire. A cowman runs on a slim profit-margin."

Jennie nodded.

"He has to have lots of land because it takes a lot of land to feed one cow. An' if he has to pay taxes on that land—well, he just can't afford to stay in business, that's all."

"I'm a farmer now. My father and I took up homestead rights on Strawberry. That makes you and me enemies?"

Will grinned. "A danged purty enemy," he said.

Jennie paid this no attention.

"My mother and me own Hatchet now," Will said. "Half an' half. She seldom leaves the ranch."

"Then you don't have legal deeds to your grazing land?"

"Just Squatter's Rights. That means the one who settled on the land first, owns the land. That theory was held up just last year by the Territory's Supreme Court."

THE RAWHIDE MEN

Lee Floren

MANOR
BOOKS
INC.

A MANOR BOOK

Manor Books, Inc.
432 Park Avenue South
New York, New York 10016

ISBN: 0-532-15399-5

Chapter One

Young Will Cooper pulled his bay bronc to a jarring halt. He stared at the girl sitting on the ground. Man alive, she was a beauty!

She had glistening red hair that tumbled down to her shoulders. She had blue eyes, and right now those blue eyes were angry. Her gingham dress had slid up to show her knees and thighs. She had very pretty legs, Will Cooper immediately noticed.

She saw where Will's gaze was directed and hurriedly pulled down her dress, but it was not long enough to cover her knees.

Will noticed the right knee was badly skinned.

"Quit staring," she said angrily, "and say something, you dumb cowpoke!"

Will didn't cotton to the word *dumb*, but he held back a hot retort. She was a stranger to him and he judged her to be either the wife—or the daughter—of one of the new nesters who'd moved in recently to homestead choice parts of his Hatchet range—usually fencing in a necessary and long-used water-hole. And water on this desert range was worth its weight in gold.

Will looked at the team and spring-wagon about two-hundred feet away. The team had evidently run away, he figured, and pitched this redhead to the ground, and thus the skinned knee.

The team had its lines tangled in the brush and could go no further. Now, the two horses stood in docile silence, absently switching flies. His glance told him they were all right.

He looked back at the redhead. She was much better looking than a team of old horses, he decided.

"Help me to my feet, you staring cowpuncher!"

Her voice held authority. It rankled Will. He looked about, as though looking for a third person. They were in the chaparral along a coulee. The girl studied him.

"What're you looking for? Or who are you looking for?"

"I jus' wanted to make sure nobody was aroun' to hear you give me orders like that," Will said.

White teeth bit a bottom lip. "I'm sorry. I guess I'm upset and my ankle—the right one—But why wouldn't you want anybody to overhear our conversation?"

"With you givin' me orders like that, the listener might think we were married."

"That's not a bit funny, Mister Cooper."

Will said, "You know my name? How come?"

"You were pointed out to me last Saturday in town."

"You a farmer's daughter?"

"I am. My father and I settled last week on Strawberry Springs."

Will almost winced. Strawberry Springs was one of his best water-holes. It ran a stream of water—not too big a stream—all the year around when some of the other springs watering Hatchet cattle went dry, during the Arid season. These nesters were becoming a serious problem.

But he said nothing about the Springs. This wasn't the time or the place to discuss such a point. This girl plainly needed help. He went out of saddle and dropped his reins, thereby ground-tying his bronc.

"What can I do to help you, Miss—?"

"Miss Jennie Clark," she said. "Get me to that root over there—on that big tree—the root exposed from the ground—I can sit there and we can take off my shoe."

Will's right arm encircled her small waist. She was warm and soft and he quickly noticed she had curves in the right places. He was still somewhat mystified.

It wasn't every day that a cowpuncher heard three dull shots signifying help, rode over the hill and into a circumstance like this.

She had an arm around him and she leaned her weight on him as she hobbled to the root, favoring her right ankle. Will had noticed a Marlin .22 single-shot rifle lying beside her and he figured that had been the weapon she'd fired to bring help.

"What were you doin' out here?" he asked.

"Picking—chokeberries," she said through pain. "I've got almost a tubful in the spring-wagon. I certainly hope they're not spilt. I tied a canvas over the tub but the way those old horses ran—You'd think each

7

was trying out for the Kentucky Derby!"

"What scared 'em?"

"Nothing that I could see. They ran away because they had a chance when I didn't hold the reins tight as I got into the spring-wagon. When they lurched the wagon ahead, my foot slipped off the door-step and I fell—and they ran."

"The oldest horses—the tamest—are the ones that run away the most," Will said. "They wait for the chance and when it comes—they're gone. I believe they enjoy a runaway."

"These sure did. They put their tails in the air and— Oh, my ankle. I sure hope it isn't broken!"

"Can I take off your shoe?"

"Please do."

Her shoes were almost new—just scratched here and there, Will noticed. They were the high-laced shoes now very popular, the mail-order catalogue had said.

"My ankle—it's swelling fast. I sure hope you don't have to cut them because—"

She stopped speaking. Will Cooper knew why. She almost admitted these were the only dress-up shoes she had.

Will knew that many of the farmers were operating on a shoestring. Money to them was very, very scarce, he'd heard. Thus, the meager investment she had in these shoes was very important to her. She'd probably have these shoes as dress-shoes for years and years, he reckoned.

He fell to both knees and began unlacing. A few hours before he'd roped and thrown a calf that had been limping on its nigh front leg.

The calf had had a sharp pointed stone jammed between the two parts of its hoof. Will had pulled the stone free with his saddle-pliers. The wound was infected and already flies had laid eggs on it.

He'd cleaned the wound out with his jackknife, the tied-down calf bawling for help, his mother circling with horns low—but never quite having the *bravo* to charge.

Will had then doctored the wound with axle-grease he always carried in a small can in a saddle-bag. The grease would keep the flies out until the abscess healed.

He now had his hands on another leg. This one, though, was not the hairy, bony leg of a calf, but the soft rounded leg of a pretty female, human. This had happened very fast. When he'd handled the calf's leg, not even in his wildest dreamings would he have imagined he'd soon be handling a female leg.

The shoe seemingly had a few miles of lacing. He pulled through one eyelet, then another. Finally, the lacing was free.

He gave the shoe a slight pull. It was firmly attached to the foot. "My ankle is swelling very fast," Jennie said.

"Can I give it a sudden an' hard pull?"

"I'll brace myself."

Will Cooper did just that. The shoe was rapidly becoming too small for her swelling ankle. He hoped the ankle wasn't broken. If so, pulling it as he would have to do to remove the shoe, would not be good.

"Again," he said.

She nodded, teeth gritted, tears of pain in her blue eyes. This time, Will got the shoe free. The ankle immediately puffed out.

"Do you think—it's broken, Will?"

Will found pleasure in the fact she'd not called him Mister Cooper, but Will. They were getting along splendidly, he figured, despite their poor start. For some very apparent reason, he wanted to become good friends with this girl—more than friends, maybe?

Will's rope-scarred thumb gently explored. "When a horse of mine broke his hock I could feel the edge of the broken bone, but I can't feel none of your ankle."

"Don't compare my ankle with a horse's, please."

"You're a frosty one."

"Frosty? What does that mean in border language?"

"Uppity," Will said.

"I don't agree with you."

Will let it stand at that. He remembered Jennie saying she'd been located on Strawberry Springs. With barbwire around Strawberry, his Hatchet cows would have to walk four miles west to Carrizo Springs—and mebbeso Carrizo had nester wire around it by this time?

He'd already noticed she wore no wedding ring. He almost asked her who was with her on Strawberry but didn't. You didn't ask too many questions in this Arizona—Sonora country.

When people wanted to tell you something, that was their business. If they didn't want to tell, it was none of your business.

"You set here," he said, "an' I'll get your team straightened around."

Jennie Clark smiled. "I'll have to sit, because I can't walk."

Will went through the chamise and sage to the spring-wagon. The reins were tied together. They'd fallen over a chamiso root and jerked the team to a halt.

They'd been jerked back hard on their haunches, scuff marks in the sand told him. If the reins hadn't been tied they'd probably still be running, he figured.

He gave the two horses—both geldings—a brief inspection. The two black had a few gray hairs interspersed in their coats.

He judged each to be around nine, give or take a year

or so.

The harnesses were old with various parts—the bellybands, the tugs—showing the heads of copper rivets put in to keep the parts together. Evidently the Clark's had bought a broken-down team of horses and harnesses for as cheaply as possible.

The spring-wagon also showed signs of age and wear. He glanced at its running-gear as he untangled the reins. The running gear was good, though—no bailing-wire holding it together.

He freed the ribbons, climbed onto the high spring seat, clucked to the team and the horses turned right in the brush toward the girl, their run completely gone. He stopped before Jennie, still sitting on the exposed live-oak root. He got down and tied the lines around a spoke in the nigh wheel.

"Why did you tie the lines like that?" Jennie asked.

Will explained. With the lines tied to a spoke, the wheel would turn if the horses decided to runaway again. "That would tighten the lines an' jerk the horses on their—" He hesitated. "Well, jerk them to a stop, Jennie."

Jennie smiled despite pain. Will knew that she knew he'd just about allowed a slip of his tongue. Will got the impression there was a lot of woman—good woman—here. "My father—He'll be wondering why I'm so late getting home."

"You got a mama?" he asked.

"Dead for years. My father raised me, you can say." She studied her ankle. The swelling had stopped but the ankle was very large. "You have only your mother, I understand."

"Where'd you hear that?"

"Gossip among the farmers."

"Just my mother," Will said. "My dad built

Hatchet. Trailed in longhorns acrost the desert from aroun' Lubbock, up in the Texas Panhandle. Years ago, before I was hatched."

"Your father—? He's dead?"

"Two years ago. Just went to sleep one night an' in the morning—he was gone."

"I'll bet you miss him."

Will shrugged. "Things like that happen." This was getting too confidential. She was still a nester. He was still boss of big Hatchet spread. Her barbwire at this moment might be making a thin Hatchet cow with wobbly-legged new calf walk miles distant for another water-hole.

Naturally, he missed Abe Cooper. He and his father had been more like brothers than father and son. He'd come late to Abe and Anna Cooper. They'd long given up thoughts of having a son—or daughter—when he'd come into sight, his dad had many times joked with him.

But that was his concern, and his alone. So he said, "I'll help you into the rig, Miss Jennie."

"I'll do my best. Will."

Chapter Two

Jennie's first concern was her chokecherries. When she saw the tarp had kept them from spilling, her eyes lighted. "I wish I knew more about cooking chokecherries," she said.

"I know all about them," Will said. "When I was a kid and even now, I sometimes get off my horse an' fill up on 'em until it looks like I have no teeth."

"They blue the teeth, they tell me."

" Just for a while. Don't stay long. When a kid smiles or talks when eatin' them, it looks like he's got no front teeth. How come you weren't eatin' 'em when you picked 'em? Your teeth are white."

"A farmer, who'd been here longer than we have, told me my teeth would stay black."

"He doesn't know what he's talkin' about." Will pulled back his lips and showed her his teeth. "I've eaten chokecherries for years—every time they've been in season—and are my teeth black?"

Jennie looked. "Definitely not."

Will turned his attention to the team and road. They were driving down a sand-wash toward the main road stretching from the Hatchet outfit to the town of Gila City, the local trading post—in which every building belonged to Hatchet. His father had built the town, every building, years ago to have a trading post close to, but not at, the mighty Hatchet spread.

The horses again wanted to stampede. Will held them in with stern reins. Had he been alone, he'd have let them run. He'd have stood in the box and hammered them with a blacksnake whip for more speed and run them until they dropped—or nearly went under.

That would have taught them a lesson they'd never have forgotten. He'd done it before with teams that itched to runaway.

His horse was tied behind the spring-wagon. He kept the team at a walk so he would not jar his injured passenger.

They reached the main wagon road. He reined the work-horses west toward Strawberry Springs, five miles away.

The road was thick with dust. Until the farmers had come a few months ago this had not been a road—it had been merely a trail. For seldom did Hatchet take a rig into Gila City.

Only once a year—in the spring—did a Hatchet

wagon go over this road. That high wheeled roundup-wagon went to Gila City for the ranch's year-supply of necessities—grub, nails, horseshoes, and things such as that.

These items came from the Cooper Mercantile, having been freighted to Gila City from Tucson, miles north.

Each spring the big wagon served as calf-branding roundup-rig. Each fall it lumbered out as the round-up wagon for Hatchet's beef-gather.

But farmer's wheels had sure loosened the sand. It lifted in clouds under the spring-wagon's narrow-rimmed wheels.

For once, Will was happy that the wind blew end-lessly on this high mountainous-desert, for the wind whipped the dust east, not allowing it to rise.

Jennie looked at the northern mountains, dim blue lines against distance. South lay more blue mountains.

"Those southern mountains—They're in old Mexico, aren't they?"

"Sonora," Will said.

"I know very little about ranching. I came from a city, you know. But the air here—clean and pure and you can see for miles."

"I've lived all my life in this basin," Will said. "I've only been out a few times, and then to Los Angeles with Hatchet cattle. That town stinks. The air there is anything but pure."

"Tell me about Hatchet?"

Will reined sharply to miss a chuck-hole. "Hatchet's a big long brand—runs the whole nigh side of a critter except for horses. We brand a small shoulder brand on our horses, so as to not ruin their looks."

Jennie nodded.

"Sometimes I wire-brand an exceptionally nice-lookin' bronc. That means we heat a thin wire and brand him under the mane where it won't show. He looks like slick, but he ain't."

"I don't understand all that, but go ahead."

"Hatchet came from Texas—the Panhandle, south of Lubbock—about thirty-five years ago, trailin' in its base stock."

"Why did it leave Texas?"

"Will hesitated, then said, "Farmers drove it out. Windmills an' barbwire. A cowman runs on a slim profit-margin."

Jennie nodded.

"He has to have lots of land because it takes a lot of land to feed one cow. An' if he has to pay taxes on that land—well, he just can't afford to stay in business, that's all."

"I'm a farmer now. My father and I took up homestead rights on Strawberry. That makes you and me enemies?"

Will grinned. "A danged purty enemy," he said.

Jennie paid this no attention.

"My mother and me own Hatchet now," Will said. "Half an' half. She seldom leaves the ranch."

"Then you don't have legal deeds to your grazing land?"

" Just Squatter'sRights. That means the one who settled on the land first, owns the land. That theory was held up just last year by the Territory's Supreme Court."

"Yes, so I've heard—a court controlled by Arizona cattle—and sheepmen."

"A person hears lotsa things," Will said.

He wasn't going to argue the point. Although Hatchet paid no taxes on the land its cows grazed over, it did pay territorial taxes on each and every head of

Hatchet cattle.

This ran into quite a sum a year. Other big Arizona cattlemen, of course, also paid high cattle-taxes. Arizona Territory's income came from cattle and sheep and timber.

So far Hatchet hadn't moved against the settlers. In other parts of the cow-country, some cattlemen and their cowboys had ridden against the nesters with rifles and side-guns.

Some nesters had been killed. Some cowpunchers had bit the dust, too. But so far it was about even-steven, Will had read in stockman journals. Somewhere the nesters won. Somewhere the cow people won.

He'd held back because of two people—his old mother and his dead father, for well did he remember Abe Cooper's words.

"Farmers will never make a go of it in Mussampa Basin, son. We only get aroun' eight to ten inches of rain a year—if thet much—an' usually it comes at the wrong time for when a farmer'd want it."

"It isn't far to water, dad. An' if they sent down wells—"

"That'd do no good. This water is full of gypsum an' alkali. You know that yourself. A new galvanized pail turns brown in less than a week."

"An' that water wouldn't raise crops?"

"It'd kill the crops. It'd put alkali an' gypsum in the soil, an' choke off the roots of wheat an' other head crops. I've tried to raise wheat an' oats. Jus' an experiment. I watered it from the well. Well, your mother ain't got no garden, has she?"

"Won't grow."

"An we got a better ally even than them things on our side, an' it's black alkali.'

17

"What's that?"

His father had explained. You could see white alkali. It lay crusted on the surface of the soil. Water brought it to the top, but black alkali was deep in the soil and when watered it turned white, too.

"But black alkali soil looks the color of good Panhandle loam, son. But it sure ain't. I've experimented with that, too. This whole range—coulees, canyons, mesas—is saturated with it. It will never be farmland. Nesters might come, but don't waste manpower an' lead fightin' them—black alkalie will have them all packin' inside of a year."

Now Jennie broke into Will's thoughts with, "Is there always wind here like this—night and day?"

"Yes, and sunrise and sunset. It never stops. But this is a mild wind. Wait until it gets the notion to blow some day."

"I hate it."

"Dad said when plows break this land it will all blow away. He said that when him an' his cowpunchers first trailed in Hatchet cattle the herd was so big it ground the brush to nothin,' an' the wind blew a big channel where the cattle had come in."

"You mean that your father said this land would never be farming land?"

"You're right, Jennie. An' then there's black alkali, too."

"Black alkali? I thought all alkali was white?"

Will explained.

She stared ahead. "Do the farmers know this?"

"Not unless Fred Bashell an' Mike Arnaiz have told you, an' I don't think either of 'em would do that—even if they knew, which I figger they don't."

Fred Bashell was the local land-locator. For a fee, he shipped in farmers and located them on homesteads.

He had come into Gila City a few months after Abe Cooper had died.

With him was his constant companion, Mike Arnaiz. Some claimed Arnaiz was Bashell's hired gunman, his bodyguard.

Fred Bashell had tried to rent a Gila City building. He'd been turned down, for all buildings there belonged to Hatchet and Hatchet sure didn't need a land-locator to break up its range.

Bashell had hired Mexican peons and built a small adobe office and living quarters at the end of Gila City's two-block long main street. He'd claimed, seeing Hatchet had no deed to that piece of land, that he would squat on it and file his homestead there—and in filing he might even take in all of Gila City, too, he was reported saying.

Thus, by filing a homestead, he could legally acquire Hatchet's town.

Hurriedly, Will had used his homestead rights, and while the town was in Will's name, Fred Bashell owned one-hundred-and-sixty acres abutting Gila City. On this he had his adobe living quarters and office.

Abe Cooper has wisely filed homestead entry on Hatchet's buildings, its home ranch. He'd done that right after constructing the big rock ranch-house and the many barns, bunkhouse, blacksmith shop and corrals.

Fred Bashell had located each and every family he'd imported—some ten or so now—on springs or water-holes vital to Hatchet's cattle.

"No, Mister Bashell never told us about the black alkali," Jennie said. Some farmers wonder why your outfit hasn't made a move to drive them out. Is it because of this alkali?"

Will nodded.

"You think we will all find out this is not farming land, and then leave?"

"That's right," Will said.

"I don't believe that."

"Your privilege."

"Mister Bashell says all this country needs is good neighbors and plenty of water."

"That's all they need in Hell, too."

She looked at him. "Now you're being facetious."

Will didn't know what facetious meant. This little redhead sure knew big words. She was as bossy and possessive as some of his schoolteachers. Was she a former schoolteacher?

He was on the point of asking when Jennie said, "It's only a mile to the homestead. Maybe I should drive in alone, Will?"

Will knew what she meant. He'd never met her father. Some of these bohunks, he'd heard, were mighty touchy where a cowpuncher was concerned. They seemed to think that a cowpuncher violated every woman he found along on the range, or some equally loco idea.

"Don't you have any brothers or sister?"

"Nope, I'm the only child. I guess you're the same, I've heard."

"You heard right. Sometimes I wish I had a brother or two—an' a sister or two—but my father said he was lucky to have me, comin' so late as I did."

"Sometimes I think being the only one is good, and then I think it's bad. Maybe I kept my father from re-marrying and living a full life," she said.

Will idly wondered if marriage meant a *full life*, as she called it. He couldn't remember when Anna Cooper hadn't harped on good-natured Abe.

Abe had grabbed his Stetson and his bronc and fled

out on the range many times to escape his wife's needle-pointed tongue.

Will stiffened inwardly. No honyocker farmer was running him around. "Somebody might have seen us out there," he said. "They'd tell your father. With me sneakin' off, you're dad would naturally think the worse."

"But we saw nobody, Will, and nobody saw us."

"You can't tell," Will said. "This brush is awful high. The world is full of pryin' eyes, even in this wilderness."

"My father—He drinks and awful lot—one reason I had him go west—Since mother died—"

"I'm drivin' you home," Will said shortly.

She looked at his stern face. "Pride?"

Will nodded. "Nobody's pushin' me aroun'," he said.

Jennie nodded. "I believe you. But I think you're bound for trouble, Will Cooper—and I'm going with you to trouble."

"We'll see," Will said.

Strawberry Springs lay at the base of a high eastern hill. The rig and occupants topped this rise, the green-ery of the Springs a splash of living color against the gray sand and pale ghost-trees.

"Down hill we go," Will said.

Jennie had no reply.

Chapter Three

A quick glance around told Will Cooper that as farmsteads go, this one was a mite less than nothing. The Clarks had dug out the side of a hill and lived in this. A canvas tarp propped up on willow poles covered the front and gave some semblance of shade.

Barbwire encircled Strawberry Springs. Will's heart sank. One of his best water-holes was gone. A half dozen Hatchet cows and calves stood beyond the six wire fence, bawling and wanting water.

"Why did you fence in the water?" he quietly asked. "You have no need for that much water."

"Yes, we do. We irrigate my garden."

"Garden?"

"Yes, I planted it right after we got here."

Will looked about. "Where is it?"

"Inside the fence."

Will then saw the rows. Spring water had been diverted to run between them. He noticed no plants had stuck their heads up. He also noticed that the space between the rows was showing streaks of white, plainly alkali. The water was bringing the black alkali to the surface and making it white, as his father had predicted.

"Nothing has sprouted yet," Jennie said, "and that's odd. The seeds have been in the ground long enough to be a few inches high, by now. Back in Ohio, you just stick a seed in the ground in the spring and in no time you have peas or beans or carrots."

"This isn't Ohio," Will pointed out. "This is the Arizona desert. There's an old sayin' that everything on the Arizona desert either bites you or sticks you. I see the black alkali is showing up."

"That white stuff there—between the rows where the water has been? That isn't black. That's white."

Will explained.

"I find that hard to believe," Jennie said. "I think that is only a residue, or something in the soil."

Will said no more. A few chickens were squated under the shade of a chamisal bush to escape the heat. Evidently the Clarks had no dog. Will knew why. A dog demanded food. Even if you shot jackrabbits and fed him these, the jackrabbits would need cartridges to kill

23

them—and cartridges cost money.

Something up slope on the hill behind the dug-out attracted his attention. He then noticed two horses there, tied under the shade of a big pepper tree. His heart sank.

He recognized them as the horses of land-locator Fred Bashell and his gunman, stolid Mike Arnaiz. He figured that the two were in the dug-out with Jennie's father.

He pulled the team to a halt in front of the canvas over-head flap. He went down with, "Well, here we are, Miss Jennie. I sure hope your ankle ain't broken."

He helped her down, fully aware of the danger he'd driven into. He heard footsteps behind him. He turned and faced a tall, thin man with sandy-colored hair and light blue eyes.

"My father," Jennie said. "The team ran away, Father. I was thrown to the ground and my ankle—I can't walk. Mister Cooper, my father, Smith Clark."

Will held out his hand. Clark made no effort to shake it. Will doubled his fist, wanting to smash the arrogant man in the face—and then he caught the odor of whiskey on Clark's breath.

The man had a breath that would scorch a fresno's steel bottom. Will dropped his hand, holding his temper. By refusing to shake hands, Clark had the same as told him he had no use for him.

Clark had given Will Cooper one of the rangeland's greatest insults. Will noticed that Jennie's eyes became angry again. Her lips drew down hard and stiff, like they'd been when he'd ridden up on her and gawked at her lovely thighs.

While Jennie explained to her father what had happened, Will went around to the back of the rig to untie his horse.

"You could have druv home alone!" Smith Clark spoke in a loud voice. "I don't like havin' my only daughter—my only get—meetin' strange men out in the hill—to me, it ain't fittin' an' proper!"

"It was all an accident, Father," Jennie pleaded. "Nothing wrong happened and I had to have help. I shot the .22 three times. I heard you say that was the signal here in this country when a person needed help. Mister Cooper happened to be over the hill—"

"How come he was on the other side of a hill? You two never arranged this meetin', huh?"

"We certainly did not! This is the first time we've ever met! You shouldn't think such things of your daughter, Dad."

Will wanted to interrupt but he decided Jennie could handle this better than he, so he was ready to mount when two men came out of the dug-out behind Smith Clark. He put his boot on the ground, standing beside his horse, looking at Fred Bashell and squat Mike Arnaiz.

Smith Clark looked at Will Cooper. "You hearin' me, Cooper?"

"I sure can't help but hear," Will said dryly. "You're hollerin' so loud you scared the chickens from the shade."

"Don't git funny with me, cowman."

Will saw then he couldn't avoid trouble. He couldn't allow the small shoulders of Jennie to bear all this burden.

"You're talkin' too much, Clark," Will said.

Before Clark could answer Fred Bashell said unctuously, "Please don't pick trouble with him, Mister Cooper. You can see he's been drinkin' too much."

Will looked at the land-locator, hate surging into his eyes, tightening his lips.

"You're awful polite today," Will pointed out.

"A lady is present," Bashell said.

Will smiled. Bashell was playing all his cards. He was trying to make a good impression on Jennie—attempting to play the role of a gentleman of the first water, Will realized.

Bashell spoke to Jennie. "Sure glad you only got a sprained ankle, honey."

Jennie studied the land-locator with cold eyes. "Since when did I become your *honey*, Mister Bashell?"

"Well, I think a lot of you and—"

"How did you know my ankle was sprained and not broken?"

"You've got your weight on it," Fred Bashell said, "an' if it was broken, you couldn't put weight on it."

Will spoke to Jennie. "I'll be leavin', Miss Clark. I hope your ankle gets well soon."

"Thank you indeed for your help, Mister Cooper," Jennie said. "Help me into the—well, *house*, Father?"

Smith Clark and his daughter disappeared into the darkness of the hill, Jennie with one arm over her father's shoulders as she hobbled. Will was swinging up when Fred Bashell said, "Get the hell off'n this homestead, Cooper—an' stay off, savvy!"

Will turned his horse. Bashell made a grab for Will's nigh boot. Will kicked his boot out of the stirrup. He gave the boot to Bashell—directly on the tip of the land-locator's blocky jaw.

He kicked with all his weight, off-boot anchored solidly in stirrup, both hands on the saddle-horn for leverage.

Bashell staggered back. Mike Arnaiz was in the act of pulling his gun. He never got it from leather. His boss crashed into him and to keep both of them from falling, Mike Arnaiz's hand left his holstered .45.

He grabbed for Bashell. He caught his boss and steadied him, thereby steadying himself.

Will realized he'd ridden into a trap. While Bashell had baited him, Bashell's gunman should have pulled and killed him; two against one—and no witnesses to say it had been cold-blooded murder.

Fred Bashell's wide face was livid with anger. He caught his balance and grabbed for Will's reins, catching them just behind the bit. Will's horse was held down.

Will left saddle. He did not use his gun. He did not think of his .45 at that moment. His only thoughts concerned his work-hardened young fists. And he put them to work.

But Fred Bashell had fists, too.

Will had long figured Fred Bashell to be in his early thirties. He wasn't as tall as Will Cooper, but he was heavier in the shoulders and thighs. He was quick as a big mountain-lion. And he knew how to use his fists, Will soon learned.

"Work 'im aroun' to'rd me, Fred." Will Cooper dimly heard Mike Arnaiz's strident voice. "Let me git a shot at him. Hell, I cain't shoot, man I might hit you!"

Arnaiz's words convinced Will Cooper he'd really ridden into trouble. They told him this land-locator and his gundog were decided upon one thing—kill him here and now.

Common sense told him that if he knocked down Fred Bashell, he'd be standing alone and the .45 of Mike Arnaiz would roar once or twice—and Will Cooper would be no more. Therefore, he fought in close and made up his mind that if Bashell went down he'd grab the man and hold him as a shield from Arnaiz's six-shooter.

A smashing right almost decked him. He then realized that he, and not Fred Bashell, might go down. He'd had his share of fistfights. So far, he had won them all. Fear tore through him. This one he might not win.

And this was no ordinary fight. He'd lose this one and he could lose his very life.

He tasted blood. Bashell also bled from the nose. Bashell's bottom lip was cut. Bashell stood wide-legged, hitting with all his sagging might—for both men were growing arm-weary.

Both gasped for air. Both faced sheer exhaustion. Will's shirt hung in shreds. The land-locator also was without a shirt.

Then, Will saw an opening.

Bashell's fists momentarily dropped, sheer weariness apparently loosening the man's muscles. And Will shot in a tough, overhand right.

He put all he owned behind it. He hit with all his waning strength. He thought for one moment that he had overshot Bashell's jaw. Then, he felt his knuckles smash against bone.

Bashell's eyes went blank. He tired to raise his fists. He couldn't. He staggered ahead, out on his boots.

Will caught him. He looked at Arnaiz over the unconscious man's shoulder. Arnaiz had been circling, six-shooter out, trying to find an opening for a killing shot.

Will bodily threw Bashell against Arnaiz. For the second time that day, Bashell's plunging weight almost bore Arnaiz to the Arizona sod.

Will put his head down. Boots digging, he whammed ahead, his skull catching Bashell just below the ribs.

Mike Arnaiz staggered back, Bashell in his arms. He fell on his back, his unconscious boss on top.

Mike Arnaiz's gun hand stuck out, the .45 trying to

point up at Will. Will kicked at Arnaiz's wrist. He missed. Arnaiz's trigger finger tightened. The gun pointed up at Will.

Will didn't kick the second time. He leaped with both boots on Arnaiz's wrist. The gunman screamed in pain. His fingers loosened. The gun fell.

Will hurriedly scooped the gun up. He threw it to one side. He then noticed that Fred Bashell's gun was still in his holster, despite the man's tumble.

His hand streaked down to his holster. To his surprise, he found his holster empty. Dismay filled him. Foolishly, he'd thrown away Arnaiz's gun, not knowing he'd lost his own.

A glance showed his pistol lying twenty feet away. Another glance told him that Mike Arnaiz had heaved the unconscious Bashell from him.

And Arnaiz had Bashell's .45.

Will did the only thing he could do—he dived for his Colt.

He heard Arnaiz's six-shooter roar. Dust spouted beside his head. He rolled over, his gun in hand.

Arnaiz had missed. He had a chance—a Chinaman's chance, but a chance. He came to one knee, six-gun raised. He centered the gun on Mike Arnaiz.

He stared, six-gun rigid.

Jennie Clark had come from the dug-out. The pretty redhead stood behind Mike Arnaiz.

Jennie's small hand clutched her Marlin .22, knuckles white. And the barrel of that little firearm was pressed flatly against the back of Mike Arnaiz's thick neck.

"Don't fire that pistol," Jennie said.

Mike Arnaiz hesitated.

"You shoot Will," the redheaded girl said, "and I'll kill you, Mike Arnaiz."

Legs spread wide, dragging in huge gulps of air, Will Cooper stood there, six-shooter covering Mike Arnaiz's gun on him. He had known that Arnaiz had him beat. He'd wondered why the man hadn't shot him. Now, he knew why.

Jennie Clark had saved his life.

Chapter Four

For one long terrible moment, death hung in the Arizona air. Fred Bashel groaned as he came to.

Mike Arnaiz was rigid, muscles tense, staring at Will—with Fred Bashell's six-gun in his hand, barrel pointed at Will's chest.

And Will stood straddle-legged, his gun's hammer eared back, the gun's front sight flat against Arnaiz's heart.

And redheaded Jennie, her .22 against the back of Arnaiz's head.

Arnaiz's hate-filled eyes took in Will Cooper. For one suspense-filled second, Will thought that the gunman might fire, despite the rifle at his head.

Then Jennie said, "You fire that gun, Arnaiz, and I'll kill you!" And Jennie Clark meant each and every word.

Suddenly, Arnaiz laughed shortly. "You two win," he said.

Then carefully, slowly, his dark hand opened, long fingers peeling away from the six-shooter's grip—and the gun fell to the dust. And Will Cooper began breathing again.

"Thanks, Jennie" Will said.

Jennie had no answer. She stepped back and broke the Marlin's breech. "No shell in it," she said.

Arnaiz's face darkened. He'd been tricked, and by a woman—but he had no words. Fred Bashell sat up, eyes landing on his own gun, lying a few feet away. He began to crawl toward the pistol.

Will walked forward. He pushed Arnaiz back with a hard shove of his open hand. He kicked the gun to one side. He spoke to Jennie. "Seems odd your father never horned in on this."

"He's passed out inside. He'll sleep until tomorrow morning, anyway. What's next, Will?"

"You're drivin' three people outa here."

"What three?"

"Bashell, Arnaiz an' me."

"I don't understand."

"You will."

Jennie climbed into the spring-wagon's seat. Will told her to turn the team around and point them uphill toward Gila City.

She did this. She stopped the rig and said, "I led you into a trap, Will. I didn't do it on purpose."

"I know you didn't."

Jennie smiled at him. Will realized she had her problems, too—and her drunken father was her greatest. His greatest cross was his mother. He spoke to the land-locator and his gundog.

"Raise your hands high. I aim to search you. You two are low enough to be packin' hidden guns—like them little derringers tinhorn gamblers have hid."

"I'm no tinhorn," Bashell said.

"You are to me."

He found no concealed weapons on either man. Both packed jacknives, no more. He gestured with his six-shooter. "Get in the wagon."

"Why?" Bashell asked.

"You got horses on the hill. You both pack saddle-rifles. I don't trust either of you, as far as I could throw a bull by his tail. Both of you are the type who'd shoot a man through the back, an' from ambush."

"This isn't ended," Bashell said.

Will nodded. "It won't be ended until either you two—or me—are off this range, and for good."

The two climbed into the spring-wagon.

"Sit on the seat with Jennie," Will ordered. "I'll stan' behin'."

He picked up the two six-shooters. He shoved them under his belt.

"What d' you aim to do with our weapons?" Bashell asked.

"I'll leave them at your office."

"When?" asked Arnaiz.

"Whenever I happen to be in town. I don't go into town much. Sometimes, I don't go in for over a year."

"You got my property," Bashell said.

Will grinned. "An' it'll be mine until I give it back to you, land-locator. Drive to the top of the hill, Jennie."

They reached the hill's top. Will went down and untied his bronc. He looked up at Jennie.

She looked weary. She smiled at him. Will Cooper smiled back. He liked this spunky little redhead. He hoped she liked him.

"You want them to ride back with you, Jennie? Or shall I make them walk back to their horses?"

"They can ride back. By the time they get to their rifles, you'll be long away from rifle range, won't you?"

"I'll be that."

Half a mile east, he topped a higher hill. The spring-wagon was gone. Had Jennie got herself into a bad corner by helping him?

She was a nester. He was the cowman. Naturally, other nesters would hear about her saving his life. Would they turn against her? Consider her a traitor to her own class?

Will pushed on. He and his partner's old pal, Apache Ike, had been running strays from the buckbrush when he'd heard Jennie's three shots. He had a hunch the old Apache had gotten worried about where his young boss had disappeared to—and would be backtracking to find out.

He guessed correctly.

The old cowboy was at the scene of the runaway. "What happened here?" he asked.

Will told him. Apache Ike listened carefully. When Will had finished the old man said, "Well, so it's come down to blows, finally."

"Finally," Will said.

"An' who won?" The old man answered his own

question. "Nobody won. It only made things worse.

"What will your mother say?"

Will said, "Does she have to know?"

"Word'll get to her in time. It always does."

Will said, "Ol' Abe Cooper was right." He told about the black alkali coming up white on Jennie's garden. "An' not a seed has sprouted, an' she said some seeds should have been up quite a few days ago."

"Seeds don't count right now," the redskin said.

Will nodded. "I know what you mean. One by one water-holes are goin'. Barbwire an' fence posts. An' without water, Hatchet is done. Hatchet stock will die of thirst."

Apache Ike said nothing.

"We'll get cowboys on what few water-holes there are left. Get them staked out there in the mornin', or as soon as possible."

"They won't be able to file homesteads," Apache Ike pointed out. "Thet Bashel fellow is a federal land agent. How he got the job from Uncle Sam, I don't know—but he's got the certificate framed an' hangin' on the wall in his office."

"You seen it?"

"I sure have. Walked to his office one day when he was gone. The window's dirty but I could see through the corner. An' I kin read enough to understan' all but a few big, long, high-toned words."

"An' we gotta get wells down," Will said. "We'd best get to town right now an' get some extra hands with shovels to start diggin' for water, or we're goin' to lose a hell of a lot of stock, Apache."

They turned their horses toward the east and Gila City, some four miles away across the chaparral. With calf-roundup finished some weeks ago and nothing to do until Hatchet hired them again for fall beef-gather,

Gila City would have quite a few idle hands looking for work.

For Hatchet's money kept the town's residents. Every man in town worked, at some time of the year, for Hatchet. These times occurred usually with calf-gather and beef-roundup. Some also trailed Hatchet steers north to Tucson for the railroad cars, after they'd been cut from the cows and bulls and calves during fall beef-gather.

When not employed by Hatchet the town kept alive on Hatchet beef, for each Sunday a choice beef was driven into town for slaughter and quartering among the town's citizens, most of whom were of Mexican descent.

Each month Hatchet distributed other necessities from its ranch warehouse. Thus, Hatchet natives lived better than most, with their future food supply practically guaranteed by the big *rancho*.

Will knew that the natives worried about the oncoming farmers. Would the farmers break Hatchet and stop the easy living? Some, he knew, had gone to work for the farmers a few days—cleaning out springs, stringing wire, driving down scrub cedar posts.

A few had even cut down scrub cedar and sold it to whatever farmer happened to have enough money to buy it. All were keenly aware of what was transpiring, as old lady Gonzalez had recently told Will's mother, Anna Cooper.

Old lady Gonzalez had ridden to Hatchet on her burro despite the broiling Arizona sun, even riding an ancient Spanish side-saddle, her voluminous dress half covering the ambling burro.

"*Los grangerous*—The farmers—They will put Hatchet on the *piedras*, on the rocks." She spoke in broken English and rough Border Mexican.

"They will not stay."

"Why do you say that, *patrona?*"

"Black alkali will drive them out. You should know about black alkali. You in town could not even grow a garden until my husband hauled in good surface soil from the mountains—all those miles. Now you have gardens, but when the old original soil was planted—if a seed did sprout, it soon died."

"Well do I remember."

"They will soon leave."

"They need meat. They will steal Hatchet cattle."

"We have thousands of steers. They are welcome to a few."

"They are not farmers. They are gunmen shipped in by that damned land-locator. Him an' his gunman, that ugly Mike Arnaiz."

"I said, they will soon go."

The Mexican mujer shook her dark braids. "They will cut Hatchet off from all water. Cows cannot live without water. Grass can be short and burned and they will milk the *mesquite* tree of its beans, like the deer do. But cows are like humans—without water, they soon die."

Anna Cooper had no reply.

"They work for this Bashell skunk. When he wins, they go on—there is something' else behin' all this, somethin' that does not meet the eye."

"You imagine things."

"Bashell will win Hatchet, unless Hatchet acts fast."

"I'll be dead before that happens!"

"Then your *dia del muerto* will come soon, senora Cooper. That is, unless Hatchet soon acts."

Anna Cooper's gray eyes coldly studied this heavy-set dark woman with the liquid brown eyes. Always she, the *patrona*, kept a wall between her and Gila City

37

residents.

Although she'd known this woman for many years this woman was still an acquaintance—and would always remain just that, and nothing more. And right now she was intruding.

"You do not own Hatchet, *senora*."

"You are right, *patrona*. On paper, I own not a grain of sand of Hatchet. But I am a part of Hatchet, nonetheless. Hatchet on paper belongs to you and your god son, but to us Hatchet belongs in our hearts—and the heart is stronger than mere paper."

Anna Cooper had no answer.

"Were it not for Hatchet, this section of the Territory would not be filled with people. It would be filled with the wolves and jackrabbits and coyotes and not *humanos*. Do you understand, *patrona?*"

"I bid you good day, *Señora*."

The heavy-set woman had slowly shaken her head. The *patrona* did not understand. Or if she did, she wouldn't admit the peril facing Hatchet.

So *senora* Gonzales had slowly mounted Pancho Sanchez. She had turned his long ears south toward Gila City. She had ridden on slowly, unmindful of the torrid heat, the sand and sand-fleas, and Pancho Sanchez's slow ambling gait.

She knew that Will Cooper understood Hatchet's danger—and so did the old Indian, Apache Ike.

She saw through Bashell's scheme. It lay clear and complete in her mind. Bashell wanted Hatchet. Whoever controlled water on this range controlled Hatchet.

Bashell had hired these homesteaders. To a man they were tough-looking, gun-toting renegades—except the drunken father of that pretty redhead, that Smith Clark. How he'd got tangled in with the gun-toters, she did not know. He was completely out of place. An accident had plainly happened.

What if Will Cooper dug wells? She wondered if Will new that his father had dug well after well, when Will had been a mere toddler.''

Abe Cooper had hit water at a short distance, but what sort of water had it been? *Senora* Gonzales knew.

For Abe Cooper had been more than a friend to the good-hearted Mexican *mujer*. Anna Cooper didn't know that. Anna Cooper had driven her husband away from her, by her sharp tongue and acid words.

Abe Cooper had told her much.

The wells had held only brackish water, bitter with alkali. Each had been worthless. A cow would drink the water only if forced.

The water would then give her the runs. She'd die in a few days of diarrhea, Abe had told her.

Abe Cooper had then dug two very deep wells. He'd lined the walls with stone and concrete to keep them from caving in.

His Mexican well-diggers finally went through granite, over a hundred feet down. Granite held sweet water—but not this granite. The water was just as evil at that distance as it had been at when shallow.

She'd tasted it.

Abe Cooper had had his workers throw sand into the wells and fill them to the brim. Where were they out on the desert? She did not know. She could not locate one now, with the years of sand drifting over the spots. The desert soon reclaimed its own.

You could scar the desert. You could tear it up, put it into mounds, and then the wind would go to work. In a short time, the desert would be as it was before—level and smiling and deadly.

Did Will know about the deep wells? She was sure he

didn't. Should she tell him? She smiled softly. It would do no good. What was the word of a Mexican woman against the thoughts of a stubborn young *hidalgo*?

She met Land-Locator Fred Bashell and his gundog, Mike Arnaiz, a mile west of Gila City. They were piloting a new homesteader to his homestead.

All three were on horseback.

She studied the homesteader. He was a hard-looking, bearded man of about forty. His gun was thonged, gun-fighter fashion, low on his blocky thigh. *Senora* Gonzales pulled in Pancho Sanchez on the side of the trail.

"Homesteader, huh?" Her tone held sarcasm. She directed her words toward Bashell.

"None of your god-damned business," Bashell snarled.

"Who's this Injun?" the homesteader asked.

"No damn' Injun," Bashell snapped. " 'Jus' a damn' Mex female who hasn't got brains enough to keep her big mouth shut."

"Where's your plow?" *Senora* Gonzales spoke to the homesteader.

"Ain't got none. Why'd you ask?"

"How you goin' to farm without a plow?"

Bashell cut in with, "What the hell difference does it make to you if he's got a plow or he ain't?"

The Mexican woman laughed softly. "Another man for the gun, eh, Bashell? You want Hatchet, an' real bad?"

Bashell studied her with cold eyes. Mike Arnaiz sported a small smile. Was it prompted by amusement or cynicism, or just plain boredom?

Senora Gonzales didn't know. This gunman was a riddle to her. She couldn't understand a man who killed for money.

"My business is my business, an' mine alone." Fred Bashell snapped the words.

"You are wrong. Your evil business is the concern of all on the grass. All of us are, in one sense, a part of Hatchet."

Bashell's face was white with rage. He lifted his quirt suggestively.

"You hit me, you white sonofabitch, an' if my friends don't kill you, Will Cooper an' Apache Ike will."

She pulled her voluminous dress high as her hand went under it to around her waist, where she grasped the smooth butt of a Smith and Wesson .32 that Abe Cooper had given her as a birthday present, years ago. Her knees and thighs showed.

Fred Bashell studied her legs. He wet his lips. "You got a gun up there?"

"Maybe I have. Maybe I haven't. But you try to hit me with that quirt, an' you'll soon find out whether I have or not."

Bashell's eyes were still on her thighs. Mike Arnaiz watched her legs with cold indifference. Arnaiz's eyes moved from her thighs to his boss's face. What he saw there made him once again smile.

This time, she could read his smile. It held cynicism and contempt. Arnaiz looked across the miles of *chamise,* sand and smoke-trees toward the northern mountains, over a hundred miles away, but blue lines in the dancing heat.

The homesteader sat a silent, thoughtful, watchful saddle, his eyes also on her full thighs.

Bashell said, "You're a smart one, Missus Gonzalez."

The *senora* did not answer.

Bashell said, "I understan' you live alone. You ain't got no man. What would you charge for a night with you?"

"Five thousan' dollars, gold."

Bashell studied her. "You're loco. You mean that?"

"I mean it."

"Bashell grinned. He looked at Mike Arnaiz. Arnaiz still studied the far mountains. He looked at the new homesteader.

"Let's go," he said.

The three loped west.

Chapter Five

Three days later, Will and Apache Ike were riding through the heat toward Gila City when quite by accident they met Sheriff Emil Dickson riding north, apparently heading for Hatchet.

"Yonder west a few rods in thet arroyo are some smoke trees," the lawman said. "Let's go there an' palaver in the shade a while, gentlemen."

Soon, they were afoot and squatting on the sand under a gray smoke-tree's welcome shade.

Sheriff Emil Dickson was pressing sixty, Will

judged. He was gaunt, stoop-shouldered—the typical cow-country sheriff with worn cartridge-belt holding a worn leather hoster that carried a worn .45 Colt, a string tied over its top just behind the trigger to keep it from jouncing from leather.

Dickson had been a long-time friend of Abe Cooper's. He had held Will on his knee. He was a firm, just man—a good lawman. You could be his best friend—or his blood brother—and if you needed to be thrown into jail, into jail you'd go.

Never did the lawman let friendship become familiarity. Apparently, he'd learned early in life the truth of the axiom that familiarity breeds contempt.

Will knew the sheriff had something important on his mind, or he'd not asked for this parley. Will and his Apache companion waited. Dickson went through brief preliminaries: He'd ridden south to the U.S. and Mexican border a week ago, on request of the United States officials at an entry port.

"They reported a few head of cattle goin' south across the border without a permit," the gaunt sheriff said. "Why they called me down was because they had a new boss there—one just out of Washington—and he didn't know what to do."

"Who's cattle were they?" Will asked.

"Hatchet's," Dickson said.

"Where abouts on the border did they enter Mexico?" Will asked.

Sheriff Dickson told him. Will nodded absently. Apache Ike had an Apache cousin who, years and years before, had jumped the San Marcos Reservation up in north-central Arizona.

The cousin had escaped into Mexico. There'd he'd gone into the cattle business with Hatchet cows. When he needed new breeding stock, he just headed north and

44

drove Hatchet cows south.

Sometimes he paid. Other times, Will just accepted the fact. Will or Abe Cooper never dunned him. He was good Mexican insurance. Were some rustlers to steal Hatchet cattle on the U.S. side and drive them into old Mexico, Will and Hatchet would be instantly notified.

"I got a lot of cows," Will said, "an' I expect some to kick an early death, unless rain comes soon an' makes water-holes."

"What's wrong with your springs?" Sheriff Dickson asked.

Will dug into his pocket, took out a sulphur and tossed it to Apache Ike, who caught the match in mid-air, drew it across the palm of his hand, and lit his wheat-straw cigaret.

Will grinned. "Come again, sheriff," he said.

The sheriff spoke to Apache Ike, "Throw me the makin's, please?" he began building a cigarette. "That's one reason I was headin' for Hatchet. In my business, a man has to be prepared—he has to look ahead. So, I did just that, an' here are my findin's."

"Recite 'em," Will said.

The sheriff had looked up the past records of Fred Bashell and Mike Arnaiz as bewst he could. "Records are mighty sketchy. I got most of my information out of the Interior Department in Washington."

Fred Bashell was a registered U.S. land-locator with a license from Uncle Sam. He always worked with Mike Arnaiz behind him.

"Bashell first located on the Elkhorn River in Nebraska. He always settled homesteaders on important water-holes. There, he drove the N-Bar-S out of business. It almost came to gun-war between his settlers and the cow-outfit. Bashell got the state militia in before guns could start speakin'."

45

Will nodded. "How long ago was that?"

"Six years ago."

"How long did it take him to break the N-Bar-S?" Apache Joe asked.

"The big outfit went out of business, because of lack of water, in two summers. Of course, a drought helped Bashell, who then sold the waterholes to an eastern outfit, who shipped in black Angus."

"Bashell come out on top?"

"Around twenty thousand dollars they think. He then pulled the same deal on The Belle Fourche River, up in northeast Wyomin'. He put the Circle-V out of business—along with another dry spell—faster than he wrecked the N-Bar-S."

"An' then he sold the water-holes, after buyin' the homestead rights from the farmers?" Will asked.

"He did. He sold again to an eastern bunch. Made around thirty thousan' or so on this deal. Then he took a few years vacation, I think—anyway, I can find no record on him, until him an' Arnaiz turned up here."

"Any killin's involved?" Will asked.

"There were three in Nebraska and four in Wyomin', but he was concerned in none, records show. His farmers all fought them. Five farmers got killed and two cowboys."

"Arnaiz?" Apache Ike asked. "He in any of the killin's?"

"He was suspected of two dead men shot from the brush, from behin'; but nothin' could be proved—so both Bashell an' Arnaiz cannot be touched by the Law, for there's nothin' against them."

Apache Ike's smoke was again dead. Again, Will Cooper tossed him another sulphur.

"Bashell's smart," the sheriff continued. "With each contract a would-be farmer signs, there's a clause in fine print sayin' the homesteader, if he sells his homestead entry, has to sell it to only one person, an' that's Fred Bashell. That don't sit good with the bigwigs in Washington, I understan' from the undertone of one letter."

"Wonder Uncle Sam allows it," Will said.

Sheriff Emil Dickson shrugged. A covey of buzzards circled north a few miles, wheeling through the lifeless blue sky. Will noticed they were gradually working their way down.

Something was dying in the brush below and the buzzards were waiting, Will knew. Probably an old Hatchet cow. This drought was eliminating some of his older she-stuff. He'd have trailed out the old cows last fall, but there'd been no market for them. Shipping them to the Los Angeles market wouldn't have paid their freight, let alone anything for their meat.

Will looked back at the sheriff. "Well, what's the verdict, sheriff?"

Sheriff Dickson got to his boots. "I'm doin' nothin', boys. Hell, there's nothin' I can do. I can't issue a warrant until a crime is committed and witnesses are there to prove it, you know."

Will and Apache Ike got to their feet, too.

"If somethin' lawless occurs," the sheriff said, "send me a written account, takin' in both sides, an' the list of witnesses names for me to talk to, if it pulls me out of the county seat." He swung into saddle, a small smile touching his lips. "That is, if it's important enough, men."

Will understood. So did Apache Ike. Sheriff Dickson was literally washing his hands of this trouble. It was up to the two factions involved to settle it by themselves. Only if the gunsmoke got thick enough to attract territorial attention would the lawman interfere—and he had doubts that would ever occur.

The Territory was a damn big area.

"Drop in and see my mother," Will invited.

"Sorry, but ain't got the time," the sheriff said.

Will and Apache Ike continued on toward Gila City. Apache Ike grinned and said, "I got a kick outa you invitin' him to visit your mama. That man ain't been in your parlor since your dad died.

"He never was a great admirer of my mother," Will said. "She bawled him out when I was a little kid, for spillin' ashes on the rug or some such useless thing."

Gila City consisted of perhaps a hundred souls, most of them Mexican descents. Chickens clucked in the dust and scrawny dogs twitched with fleas and flies and heat, in the shade, ribs showing.

Fred Bashell's new office was on the outskirts of town. The door was closed and Will leaned low and called, "Hello, the house," but got no answer. He had the guns of the land-locator and his gunman in a sugar sack.

"Nobody home," Apache Ike said.

Will threw the sack through a window. Glass cascaded and the guns landed on the cement floor inside.

"Bashell will like that broken window," Apache Ike said.

"One way to cement a friendship," Will said. They rode to the Hatchet town livery-barn run by all two-hundred-and-sixty pounds of Pedro Morales, who sat on an old chair by the door, sound asleep.

Will's .45 lifted. His bullet hammered dust over Pedro's old boots. Pedro leaped from the chair, hands automatically rising shoulder high. Every dog in town came awake. Every dog barked.

"Oh, it is you, *patron*," Pedro said, upon seeing Will. "I see you are still alive, *senor* Apache Ike."

"I'll dance at your funeral," the redskin said.

Pedro crossed his massive bare chest. "It is for *Dios* to determine that, not us mere men." He looked up at Will. "I was chasin' a blonde woman when your gun went off by mistake."

Will swung down, Apache Ike following suit. Will looked down the two blocks of the main street. People had come from the adobes at the sound of his gunfire. A few had come onto the saloon porch. He recognized the bartender and Fred Bashell and Mike Arnaiz.

The land-locator and his gunman each had a whiskey glass in hand. Will ironically lifted a hand to them. The bartender waved back, but Bashell and Arnaiz didn't.

"They do not like you," Pedro said.

Will handed Pedro the reins. "Grain an' feed them after waterin' them," he said. "Why wouldn't Bashell an' Arnaiz like me?"

"From what you did to them a few days ago at Strawberry Springs."

"They tell you about the ruckus?"

"No, but the farmer—that Clark—he got drunk an' told all. He just left town. His daughter came in after him."

Will said, "Wish I could have seen her. Danged nice little heifer." He looked at Juan Delgado, an old *amigo* of his father. "How are you today, *senor* Delgado?"

"I was huntin' cottontails in the brush," the old man said. "Back of the *oficina* of *senor* Bashell. Whatever you threw in there missed the door. It went through the window, instead—an' the window is in many, many pieces."

"You mean—I missed the door?" Will asked.

"The door was closed."

Will looked at Apache Ike. "Think of that. My eyes

49

are really bad. I thought I threw those guns through the open door, an' Juan here says they went through the window. And broke it, too."

"You don't say," Apache Ike said.

Juan said, "You are loco. Both of you. A sensible person would leave this town this minute."

"Why?" Will asked.

Juan said, "I will talk with my missus about leaving." He turned and went down the shady side of Main Street. Will and Apache Ike went to the saloon. They'd just climbed the few sagging steps to the porch, when Fred Bashell and Mike Arnaiz came out the swinging doors.

Will and his companion stopped, with Apache Ike discreetly moving a few paces from his boss. Will noticed that both Arnaiz and Bashell now had guns in their holsters.

"Rooted out some new arms, eh?" he said.

Neither man spoke. Will looked at Bashell's face. The man had one eye swollen shut. The other had a blue ring around it. His lips were double normal size.

Happiness surged through Will Cooper. If the winner of a fistfight were the one who escaped with the least signs of damage, he'd plainly won over Bashell.

Bashell said, "We don't want trouble, Cooper."

"I know that," Will said. "All you want is Hatchet."

Bashell looked at him from his good eye. "You're a trouble maker," he said. "Come along, Mike."

"Your guns are in your office," Will called after them.

Bashell stopped. "How'd you get them inside? The door was locked."

"The window's open."

"Window open?" Bashell asked. "I shut it just before I left. It can't be open."

"I opened it," Will said. "With the guns. Like this." He made a motion of throwing something heavy.

Mike Arnaiz had his hand on his holstered gun. Bashell saw this and said, "No, Mike, no. Not here, Mike."

"From the brush, eh?" Will said. "Some dark night, Bashell?"

The bartender and saloon swamper watched through a window, well out of possible fire. Townspeople discreetly watched—and listened—from the safety of thick-walled adobe doorways and windows.

Bashell addressed the town. "People, I am a peaceable man. I came here to settle homesteaders on land that will in turn produce money, and in turn build up this country. This man assaulted me the other day for no apparent reason. What this town needs is a lawman, a deputy sheriff or town marshall."

A heavy male voice sounded from a doorway down street. "What this town needs, mister is not homesteaders—this town needs one thing, and that's rain, an' a hell of a lot of it!"

Somewhere, a woman laughed. Will wondered if the throat laugh didn't come from *señora* Gonzales's lathery throat.

Fred Bashell's black and blue face showed sudden anger. He stood for a moment, hands clenched, looking up and down the dusty street with its one-story adobe houses; then he turned and strode toward his office, Mike Arnaiz at his spurs.

Will and Apache Ike entered the saloon. By this time Tina, the bartender, was behind the bar, the swamper sweeping the concrete floor like mad—for the boss had come in, and the boss seldom entered the saloon.

The old boss, Abe Cooper, he used to come in more often, God bless him. The *latino* swamper crossed

51

himself.

The Hatchet men ordered beer. The bar held only these four. Tina cranked the windlass lifting the beer bucket from the cold well water. His belly lurched and bounced.

Will looked at the big belly and remembered that when he'd been a mere boy his father had found Tina— then a young lad—wandering through the chaparral, more dead than alive—a refugee from Mexico. His dad had given him the job of swamping and years ago, the Tub had worked up to bartender.

When they'd buried Abe Cooper, the whole town had wept—except for Tina, who'd stood dry-eyed, staring at the open grave. When the coffin had been lowered he'd screamed and leaped on it, wanting to go to the grave with the only man he'd thought a god.

"Will," he said, "There's trouble."

"There always is," Will said. "What nature does it carry now?"

"Pronto Robbins."

Will scowled. Pronto Robbins was one of the first nesters Fred Bashell had shipped in. He had fenced in one of the Hatchet's best water-holes, Grasshopper Springs.

He'd fenced forty acres, completely cutting off Hatchet cows even from seep water. Will had ridden past Robbins' fence a week ago. Robbins had planted the forty in wheat.

Evidently Grasshopper Springs' soil held less black alkali than other spots, for the wheat had sprouted and was about six-inches high before the alkali killed it.

Had it been planted on good loam it now should have had heads and stood belly-high to a high horse, waving in the wind. As it was, the crop was worthless. It would never head-out. Will had doubted if a critter would even eat it, with so much caustic alkali in its stalks.

Pronto Robbins looked anything but like a farmer. To Will he looked like a gunfighting cowboy. Always, he had his .45's holster tied down in best Wild Bill Hickock manner. He didn't walk. He swaggered.

He was thin, about thirty five—and always his pale eyes, nestled under sandy brows, swept here, then there, then back again, as though measuring the area around him for possible enemies.

"What's Pronto's hen?" Will asked.

"He claims somebody cut his barbwire fence last night. When he woke up this mornin', his wheat field was trampled flat by cattle."

"Hatchet cattle, eh?"

"That's what he says. The cows wouldn't eat the wheat. They jus' milled aroun' an' pounded it flat, he says."

Will looked at Apache Ike. "What'd you say?"

"Bashell an' Arnaiz," the Apache said. "I was over in that area yesterday. Quite a bunch of Hatchet cows aroun' there. I wondered why so many happened to be in one place at the same time. Then I figured they'd come to try to get some water. About eight miles to the closest water, over on Mornin' Glory, Will."

"See anybody bunchin' cows?" Will asked.

Apache Ike shook his head. "But they could've seen me first an' hid in the buckbresh."

Will spoke to Tina. "Where's this Robbins bucko now?"

Robbins was in town. He'd ridden in to tell Bashell and Arnaiz of his misfortune. "I think he's in the Merc, now."

The swamper said, "He's in the Merc. I'll check to make sure, though." He hurriedly put his tule-cane broom in a corner and pulled off his apron and left.

"He was in here?" Will asked.

"Came in lookin' for you. Had a beer an' left. I figured he'd ride out to Hatchet, an' I've kept watchin' him so if he did, I could send a man out fast, circlin' ahead of him, an' warn you, boss."

"Thanks for the thought," Will said.

The swamper entered. "He's in the Merc. He's buy'n ca'tridges an' fillin' the empty loops in his gunbelt. Alfonso is tryin' to talk him into goin' back to his farm." Alfonso Garcia ran the Merc for Hatchet.

"An' he ain't drunk—or been drinkin'?" Will again asked, to make sure.

The swamper said, "Sober as an owl. I got clost to him. Smelled his breath, even. No booze on it."

"He's stone sober," Tina said.

Will said, to Apache Ike, "Then I can't dodge him."

"He might jus' be talkin'," Apache Ike's voice held worry. "An' maybe now thet he hears you're in town an' you might call him, he might get his hoss an' sneak out."

"I hope so," Tina said.

The swamper was watching from the edge of a front window. "Here he comes now," he said.

Tina said, "That's natural. His saddle-horse is tied in front of the cafe. To get to it he has to walk this direction."

Silence fell with only an occasional fly buzzing past to break it. Will and Apache Ike stood at the bar, beer bottles still almost full, with Will realizing that he had never drawn a gun against a human and fired.

He'd had lots of gun practice. Twice a year cowboys from spreads hundreds of miles away congregated in Gila City, when Hatchet held its every-sixth-month rodeo.

Invariably, Will's gun won the shooting contests. Both Abe Cooper and Apache Ike had taught him how to reach, level and draw since he was big enough to handle a pistol, his first being a small .22 revolver.

But shooting against a human—with your knife at stake—was a horse of another color, he'd been told. He found his guts tightening.

"He just' walked past his hoss," the swamper said.

He left the window. He scurried behind the bar. He came out with a double-barreled sawed-off twelve-guage shotgun. "I'm hidin' behin' that barrel in the comer," he told Will.

"Wait a minute," Will ordered.

The swamper stopped. "What's on your mind, boss?"

"You aren't thinkin' of ambushin' him, are you?"

"I will if you say so. I'll fill him so full of buckshot his top half won't know where his bottom half landed. Jus' you say so, boss."

Will shook his head. "I'll tend to him."

"You tend to him," the swamper said, "an' I'll tend to the barrel." He went behind it, shotgun and all, and disappeared.

Will and Apache Ike still stood at the bar, backs to the door, watching the door in the backbar mirror.

"He's comin' up the steps onto the porch now." Tina kept a running report. "He's almost to the door now. He's at the door. You see him in the lookin' glass, boss?"

"I see him." Will said.

Tina said, "I got a call to the can, outside. I believe I left a shotgun somewhere out the back door. Hello, Robbins. Sorry, but nature calls. Pick a bottle of whatever you want, friend."

Pronto Robbins stopped just inside the door. He

spread his legs wide, drew down into a crouch and said, "Cooper, last night Hatchet cut my fence. Hatchet drove Hatchet cows in on my wheat field. That wheat field was all I had, my money for this year's crop-an' hard work."

Will turned clearly, "I've heard of this, Robbins. But Hatchet didn't drive them cows in on your wheat. Hatchet never cut your fence. Hatchet doesn't hit in the dark. Hatchet fights above the table."

"You lie, an' you know it, Cooper!"

The words rang across the saloon's still air. To call a man a liar on this range was second to calling him a son-of-a-bitch. The words son-of-a-bitch insulted both the man and the man's mother. Calling a man a liar insulted only the man.

Will caught his anger. Something was drastically wrong here. This man had more courage than he should have had. Plainly, he'd not got it from a bottle. Then from whence had it come.

Will said slowly, "Robbins, you can't win. There's only one way you can go out of this saloon if you pull your gun—an' that's on a plank."

"I don't getcha, Cooper."

"Look at that beer barrel to your right."

"You're tryin' to trick me. I'll look an' you'll blast me."

Will shook his head. "Jus' look, Robbins."

Robbins' shot a glance at the barrel. He saw the double-barreled shotgun staring at him over the barrel's top.

Will watched closely. Will figured that sight of the shotgun Robbins would pale or show some emotion, but the man's face remained the same—bestial and smeared with the lust to kill.

Robbins' eyes returned to Will. "That might get me,"

he said, "but before it does, I'll get you."

Will said, "Look at the back door."

Robbins looked. He stared into Tina's shotgun. Again, no surprise or fear lanced his face. Will knew then he wasn't normal. Robbins's darting eyes returned to Will and then moved over to Apache Ike, who had his old hand on the butt of his holstered Colts.

Robbins wet his wind-cracked lips. He seemed to be debating something. Will and his people patiently waited. The tension had left Will Cooper. His muscles were limp but yet alert. Suspicion was strong in the young cowman. He was sure this man had something beside his arm up his sleeve.

Robbins said, "I wouldn't have a chance. This ain't the time nor the place Cooper. I'll settle with you sometime when I git you alone."

"That's a good idea," Will said.

Robbins began backing slowly toward the front door, carefully placing his boots behind him, his eyes missing nothing.

Apache Ike whispered, "Watch 'im, Will."

Will had no reply. He watched Robbins. Robbins got next to the door. He reached behind him to make sure the door was closed. Then he said, "Well, to hell with you all!"

He turned as though to leave. But he did not leave. He completed a fast circle. When he landed on spread legs, he faced Will Cooper. And his .45 was in his fist.

But Will had taken Apache Ike's advice. When Robbins whirled, Will Cooper threw his length forward, landing on his belly on the concrete floor, his .45 rising.

Robbins' bullet hit the bar behind Will. Had Will been standing, it would have hit him just above the belt. Will's .45 leveled. He took a precious second. He aimed as his father and Apache Ike had trained him years ago.

He laid his forefinger along the gun's barrel. He pointed it directly at Pronto Robbins' chest. Two times the big .45 blasted. The second shot was not needed. The first lead had done the work.

The first bullet smashed into the farmer-gunman's chest. It drove him back. It turned him, as it drove. Pronto Robbins' .45 flew from his grip. Robbins plunged through the batwing doors and disappeared. Will saw only his boots through the space under the doors.

The boots didn't point toes up. They pointed heels-up. Automatically Will found himself reloading. And to his surprise, his hands were steady.

"You remembered," Apache Ike said.

Will noticed that Apache Ike had his short-gun in hand. The bartender came back inside. The swamper and his shotgun went out a window that had no glass.

Hatchet riders had broken it by accident a few weeks ago, when a couple had gone on a drunk.

Will hostered his gun.

The swamper's words came from outside. "He ain't movin', Will. I think he's dead."

Will spoke to Apache Ike. "There was something' wrong with him. His eyes—the pupils were too wide. He wasn't steady on his boots. He must have been drinkin'."

"I don't think so," Apache Ike said.

Will, Apache Ike and Tina went outside, Tina still carrying his shotgun. Pronto Robbins lay in a small pool of blood. Apache Ike went to one knee beside the dead man.

"Roll 'im over," Will said.

Apache Ike did.

Pronto Robbins wore a vest. A Bull Durham paper tag stuck out of one of its pockets, the tag red with its owner's blood. Apache Ike's gnarled fingers went through the vest's pockets. They found nothing but the Bull Durham sack and it held not fine-grained tobacco, but small cactus buttons.

"Peyote," Apache Ike said.

Will nodded. Many of the town's natives went on peyote drunks. The cactus button grew in many yards in town and the desert was full of them. He now understood Pronto Robbins' bravado and behavior. Peyote made you live in a dream world, where everything was rosy and high and everything came out all right.

Will knew full well the strength of peyote. He'd tried it some years ago at one of *Señora* Gonzales's many *fiestas.* After finally coming back to normal, he hadn't the slightest idea of what he'd said, done or saw.

Once had been one time too many.

Townspeople had gathered around, staring and talking their rough Spanish. Young Doc Martinez pushed through with his black bag. He was but a few years older than Will.

Abe Cooper had sent Rafael Martinez through a medical course in Tucson. He'd wanted the young man to finish the school because Gila City needed a medical doctor.

But Martinez couldn't stand the study. He had quit after two years. Now, he studied medicine from books he had sent to him from various eastern publishers. Some claimed him a good doctor of medicine. Others claimed him stupid from the boots up. Will and his father had considered him a shade better than nothing.

Doctor Martinez got to his feet. "He's dead," he said.

Apache Ike said, "We figured he was," and cynicism marked his four words. Will noticed that land-locator Fred Bashell and Mike Arnaiz were in the group. Gunroar had evidently reached Bashell's distant office.

Will spoke to Apache Ike. "See if he's got any money on him."

"Okay, boss."

The redskin found fifty dollars in gold in Robbins' old wallet. There wasn't a bill or another coin in the bill-fold—only two gold double-eagles and a single eagle.

The coins were so new they glistened in the Arizona sunlight, despite the porch's roof. Will juggled them and said, "He must've just rolled them out of his money-machine."

Brown eyes watched him. Most of these people had never had a gold eagle in their lives, let alone a double eagle—and most had long ago given up hope of ever owning one or both.

Will's eyes were on Fred Bashell. "Robbins hasn't had this money on him long, I figger. Jus' a short while, maybe—'cause I think somebody paid him this to kill me."

Silence held the group.

"They got him full of peyote, first—then sent him out, these eagles in his pocket, to kill me."

Nobody said a word. The only sound was the eternal wind singing in the porch's eaves.

Will broke this with, "Maybe this gold came from up in Wyomin', locality of the Belle Fourche River?"

Eyes watched, wondering what he talked about.

"Or mebbeso from the Elkhorn River of Nebraska?" He looked fully at Fred Bashell. "Where do you think it came from, land-locator?"

Bashell wet his lips. "I haven't the slightest idea," he said.

Will said, "You're backin' down, man."

Bashell shook his head. "I'm a peaceful man. I don't know what you're talkin' about, Cooper. An', for another thing, I don't give a damn."

He turned and walked down the steps. He went around the saloon's east corner and disappeared, with Mike Arnaiz following. He was headed the direction of his office.

Will handed the gold to *señora* Gonzalez who, as usual, wore a few yards of dress that flowed in the wind. "This money goes to the school," he said, "an' you're head of the school board, so keep it until school starts again and one day give the kids a big *fiesta*." He grinned. "But leave out one thing, please."

"What's that?" *Señora* Gonzalez asked.

"Peyote," Will said.

Chapter Six

That same night Will was in the foreman's cabin working on Hatchet's books when the Cocapah squaw stuck her head in and said, "Your mama—In the house—She wants to see you."

Will scowled. He'd been in the middle of adding a long string of numbers. Now, he'd lost his count. One thing was certain—this drought had really effected the weight of Hatchet cattle.

For three years now, very little rain had fallen in Mussampa Basin. Old Apaches claimed this was the longest drought in their memory and their story-tellers told only of one drought in history this severe and that was over a hundred years ago.

And with poor cattle, small receipts came in.

"I'll be right up," Will said.

"She said right away."

"Right away," Will assured.

Squaw pulled her head out of the doorway and Will heard her moccasins shuffle south along the gravel walk. This sound then died and the wind still sang in the eaves. Down in his corral, the stallion neighed and pawed, wanting open range and mares in heat.

He'd bought the stallion in a Los Angeles auction, the first cattle-shipment to the Pacific coast after the death of Abe Cooper. He needed a bit of hot-blood in the brood mares to have them turn out colts and therefore, better and faster cutting-horses.

Will began adding again. His sum arrived at, he leaned back in his chair, and feared what lay ahead. Finally, he got to his boots, cupped a palm over the top of the lamp chimney, and extinguished the light.

It was ten o'clock. The night was hot, sultry. Overhead, a quarter-moon hung in a silent, cloudless sky. Will stepped into the hot night, wondering if it would ever rain again.

He walked slowly toward the big, long stone ranchhouse. He noticed only one light—and that a yellow glow of a kerosene lamp in the huge living room with its fireplaces on both ends.

His father had picked a good location. Abe Cooper had built the ranch-house higher on the slope, with the barns and other buildings below. He wondered, idly, how many times his father had reluctantly trod this same path upward in response to his wife's demand.

For Abe Cooper had given up living in the ranch-

63

house. He'd put his foreman into the bunkhouse and had moved into the foreman's cabin—lock, stock and barrel. And after his father's death, Will had done the same.

He'd deserted the big house. Now, Anna Cooper lived alone. He seldom entered the ranch-house, unless his mother had sent word down-hill she wanted to see him.

He crossed the flagstone-floored porch, bootheels pounding, and knocked on the heavy oak door.

"Come in."

He entered. His mother was as he expected. She wore a dressing gown—her blue one—and her gray hair was done in a severe bun. He closed the door and leaned against it and wondered why in the hell some humans could never agree. Why did some always pick the opposite side? Just to be ornery?

He thought fleetingly of Jennie Clark. He was young and women were few, and he had his young dreams. Gila City had pretty girls—Mexican girls—but the boss of Hatchet didn't marry one of his servants. He didn't even play around with them. Abe Cooper had given him stern orders. Now, with his father gone, he realized Abe Cooper had been right when he'd said that the *dueño*—the boss—lived a lonely life because he was the owner, the *patron*, the special man, the one standing at the top, and standing alone.

What if he and Jennie Clark married? Such was possible. Would they end up estranged, as had his father and mother?

"Why did you knock?" His mother asked.

Will shrugged. "I don't know."

"This is your house as well as mine. You needn't knock at your own door. Sit down, please."

Will went to the table, hat in hand. He sat down on one of the sturdy high-backed leather-seated chairs his father had had old Gustavo, a Mexican, make-years ago.

"What seems to be the trouble?" his mother asked.

Will looked at her fine-boned, thin face. She had aged much since Abe's death. Probably lonesome for somebody to fight with, he ironically thought. He had a hunch that tonight would see him boss of Hatchet, or saddling a horse with his warbag tied behind the cantle.

When he'd been fourteen, he'd pulled out with a trail herd heading into Montana. He'd then trailed into the Black Hills and down into Nebraska, and was gone four years.

Now, his father was dead. Hatchet had to be bossed. He said, simply, "This Fred Bashell moves farmers in on Hatchet water. Soon, Hatchet cows will have no water. Bashell is after Hatchet. At the rate he's goin', he'll own Hatchet in a year or so."

"I can hardly believe that."

Will shrugged. "Then don't." The barrier was rising again. No, it wasn't rising, he corrected; it's always been there. It's just growing higher.

He said nothing.

"Why don't you talk?" his mother finally asked.

"About what?"

"How will Bashell take over Hatchet?"

Will told about meeting Sheriff Dickinson. "Bashell will buy homestead entries from his phony farmers. He'll control all of Mussampa water. Whoever owns Mussampa owns Hatchet."

"Dig wells."

"I'm goin' try that. But ol' Jaime Ochoa said Dad tried that years ago. Ochoa said Dad got nothing but alkali water, no matter how deep he went."

"Your father never told me."

"Maybe you never gave him a chance?"

65

"Watch your tongue, son. I'm your mother. I brought you into this world. Without me, you'd not be here."

Will said, "I've heard that, god knows how many times. Jus' remember one thing, an' one only—I'll fight to my death for Abe Cooper."

"Your father's dead."

"His spirit isn't."

"Your father was a man, not a cattle-brand."

Will got to his feet. "I have to correct you. Hatchet is Abe Cooper. Abe Cooper was Hatchet."

His mother's sharp eyes watched.

"You've said time and time again, I'd not be here if it wasn't for you. I say that Hatchet would not be here if it wasn't for Abe Cooper."

She watched through scheming, lidded eyes.

"I don't care what you think. I long ago gave up tryin' to please you. Dad did the same. But I tell you this—if it looks for one instant like that damn' Bashell and that slit-eyed gundog of his are going to win, I'll move with my gun against both—even if they kill me."

"What if I order you not to?"

"I'd pay no attention to your order."

Her cold eyes watched him. Her left hand moved slightly. The diamond ring there cast out facets of light. Will remembered when his father had brought that ring back from Los Angeles. Abe Cooper had gone west with a trainload of Hatchet cattle.

"You killed a farmer today in town," she said.

Will said, "I figgered some big mouth in town would haul herself or himself out here to tell you. Yes, I killed a man—but he wasn't a farmer."

"He had a homestead."

"He was a gunman posin' as a homesteader. He had money in his pocket—gold, and he got paid that to lift a

66

gun against me."

"Your father never killed a man."

"Mebbeso he never had to."

She considered that and then said, "Go, son, go. You're a murderer. You're the first murderer that has ever been in this house."

Will stared at her. He then realized something he'd feared for some time—her mind was breaking. She was on the brink of a breakdown. For one thing, she lived alone too much. Very few women from town ever visited her. Frankly, she considered herself above them, for they were of Spanish descent or Mexican *mestizo*, mostly the latter.

Will halted at the door, hat in hand.

She said, "Why don't you buy the farmer's homestead rights? Why do you let this land-locator outsmart you? Hatchet is a wealthy ranch."

Will almost winced. She should look at Hatchet's ledgers. Then he realized that if she did look at his bookkeeping she'd probably not understand the figures, anyway.

He told of the clause each contract held, between Fred Bashell and the homesteader.

"Who told you that?" she asked.

He told her.

"Have you ever seen one of the contracts?"

Will admitted he hadn't.

"Then you don't know, for sure?"

"I take Emil Dickinson's word. I trust a friend of my father."

"Your father had some worthless friends. If you trust every bum who took advantage of your father's good nature, you're trusting a bunch of bums."

"That's my lookout."

Her next words froze Will Cooper at the door. "This

farmer's daughter—? This redheaded girl—?"

What hadn't she been told? "Do you mean Miss Clark?"

"Yes, Miss Clark. Jennie Clark. Homesteader on Strawberry Springs, they tell me."

Will knew his mother hadn't the slightest idea where Strawberry Springs was located. She'd not ridden in all these years over one acre of Hatchet range, either on horseback or in her buggy.

Abe Cooper had tried without success to get her out of the house and ride with him on circle. She'd refused.

The only Hatchet grass she'd seen was along the road leading south to Gila City. And she went to town very seldom. Right now, Will couldn't remember when she'd last been in town, it was so long ago.

"What about Jennie?" he asked.

"You've had a meeting with her. Out on the range, they tell me. You went to her homestead. You had a fight there with Bashell and Amaiz."

"You miss nothin'," Will said.

"You like her?"

"I hardly know her."

"She isn't Mexican, is she?"

Will smiled. "Not with a name like Clark," he said.

Anna Cooper said, "She shan't become mistress of Hatchet. Hatchet is my property, not hers." Will realized then, for sure, she was mentally deranged. "Go now, son, and God be with you."

"Good night, mother."

"Good night, son."

Will closed the door softly behind him, the thought coming that he couldn't remember her calling him anything but *son*, and he calling her not *mama*, or *ma*, but always the stilted *mother*.

He had a feeling that he'd crossed a bridge and the old

era was closed behind him, the bridge falling into a roaring, foam-tossed river. He knew now he was boss of Hatchet. Her wavering mental condition told him that.

He cocked his head, listening. There it was, the ever-howling wind in the eaves. Night and day, day and night. He remembered reading, a year ago in the Tucson *Register*, that ninety percent of the ranch women in Arizona who broke up mentally did so because of the always-present forever-howling Arizona wind.

He realized he knew very little about his mother before her marriage to his father. Young Will Cooper had helped trail a herd of Hatchet cattle out of the Texas Panhandle to Saint Louis, Missouri, for sale.

When he'd come back, he'd had a bride.

He'd never heard where and how his father had met his mother. The courtship must have of necessity been short, for Abe Cooper had been in Saint Louis but a few days, his father had said.

He'd never seen—or heard of—a single relative on his mother's side. He knew no more now, about his mother and her past life, than he'd known when he'd been a boy in grammar school in Gila City.

He walked down the graveled walk to the foreman's cabin. Apache Ike squatted in the dark beside the log cabin and had he not spoken, Will undoubtedly would not have seen him.

"Will."

Will's hand went to his holstered gun. Apache Ike came upright and said, "Damn, I'm sorry, son. I should have moved out into the starlight. I get more forgetful as I get closer."

"Closer to what?" Will asked.

"The last six feet," the Apache said.

Will said, "Come on inside." He didn't light a lamp. He said, "A session with my mother."

Apache Ike settled on the cot. He was silent.

Will sighed, "I believe I won."

Apache Ike said, "I got the crew lined up. We go below that Clark fence an' dig the first well. Seepage may have in years cleaned out that soil of alkali. There might be a chance there's sweet water from Strawberry."

"Clark's got forty acres fenced," Will reminded. "That's an area a quarter mile square. The Spring is in the middle. A quarter mile square is eighty rods by eighty."

The cot squeaked as Apache Ike shifted positions. "That means from the Spring to the fence is forty rods. We've got a chance, Will."

"Let's hope so," Will said.

Apache Ike got to his feet. "I got guards stationed out. Curly and Jack until midnight. Then, Wad and Henry take over until dawn. Sunrise comes early this time of the year."

Will had no words.

Apache Ike halted at the doorway. "Let's look at it from the realistic viewpoint, Will. More than Bashell an' Arnaiz want your scalp now. You killed Pronto Robbins."

"He was no farmer. He was a hired gunman, put by Bashell an' Arnaiz on a homestead as a make-believe sodman."

"How right. But...Robbins is dead, an' your gun kilt him. Makes no difference whether the killin' was justified. You an' me know it was. But the farmers never seen it."

Will accepted that.

"Bashell will tell his gunmen that Robbins didn't have a chance, with three Hatchet guns against him."

Will nodded. "Maybe some of those would-be farmers will tuck tail now an' run, seein' there's gun-

'smoke an' hell ahead, fer sure?''

Apache Ike shook his head. ''They're tough men. The only one I know of with kin is this Clark drunk, an' how he ever got into thet bunch I sure don't know. Must've been by accident, both on his part an' Rashell's.''

Will nodded.

''Bashell's payin' his gunmen good wages. He's bound to me. 'Member what Dickinson said about all the *dinero* Bashell made over in Nebraska? Yeah, an' in Wyomin', too?''

''He'll be payin' them gunfighter wages,'' Will agreed.

''For damn' sure, son.''

''We should put guards out aroun' the ranch,'' Will said.

''They're already stationed, Will. I sent 'em out. I reckoned you had so much trouble—so many things to think about—Well, I stationed 'em, knowin' it'd be okay with you.''

''Don't know what I'd do without you, Apache.''

''You'd get along. No man is ever missed when he's dead or gone. How about wells?''

''Tomorrow we, dig.''

''Won't work, son. Your father tried. He went over a hundred feet deep, an' through granite—an' only alkali water.''

''Why didn't you tell me this before?''

''Didn't find occasion to, I reckon.'' Apache Ike yawned. ''Me for the hay.'' He slept in the barn's hay-mow. Through the wide doors he could see for miles around. ''Goodnight.''

Will went to bed. Dawn wasn't far off.

Although the day had been rough he immediately fell asleep. Red dreams plagued him.

71

He went through three roaring gunfights. He killed his man each time. Then, out of nowhere, came six riflemen, Winchesters raised. He whirled to face them.

He smiled. He was lightning-fast. He had six bullets in his .45. One for each rifleman. He fanned his hammer.

He got only clicks.

His gun had no cartridges. Either that, or his ammunition was bad. He was doomed. Bullets left the rifle-barrels. He saw them coming. They would kill him.

He came startlingly awake. Happiness flooded him. It had not been real; it had been only a dream—a nightmare.

He was cold with sweat. His right hand opened and closed, damp and trembling. He was in his bed.

There had been no gunfights, no riflemen.

Then he heard old Apache Ike shout, "Gun roar, men! From back of the house, south on the hill!"

Will then realized that actual gun-shots had awakened him. He swung his legs over his bunk, grabbed his pants, pulled on his boots and hurriedly buckled on his heavy gun-belt.

Outside, sounded running boots and shouts. Apache Ike had apparently quit his high viewpoint and Hatchet riders came running from the bunkhouse. Will barged outside.

The moon was gone. The Arizona sky held fading stars, for dawn was creeping in, putting them to sleep.

"What the hell is it, Apache?"

The old man puffed. "Shootin', back of the house. Three shots, boss. Pistol shots, too."

Hatchet punchers came running, some carrying side-arms, some carrying rifles. Smoky Cotterman packed a double-barreled scattergun. Questions were asked, scanty answers given.

Will glanced at the house. A lamp had been lighted in his mother's bedroom. "Who's on guard?" He shot the question at Apache Ike.

"Henry's got north guard. Wad's got the south."

"Spread out, men," Will said. "Spread out wide, an' move ahead. There should be Wad only, on the hill."

They moved into the darkness. Apache Ike stayed close to Will. There was no more shooting. Will and the Apache got behind the house. Ahead was the steepest part of the Hill, and the hill was covered with chaparral.

Will hollered, "Wad, where are you?"

There was no answer. Fear struck the Hatchet owner. Wad was no more than a stripling, the youngest of the Hatchet riders.

"Wad, answer me, damn it!" Will hollered.

This time a voice came. "Over here, boss. There's a dead man here, Will."

"You kill him?"

"Hell, no."

Will scowled. He spoke to Apache Ike. "What the hell is this, anyway?"

"I don't know" Apache Ike said. "Sounded like he's in thet mess of ol' granite boulders you used to play Injun in, when you was a young-un."

"Come on in, men," Will hollered. "The boulder clump."

Somebody said, "Here comes Jake. He went back for a lantern."

The kerosene lantern's flickering rays showed young Wadsworth Jones bending over a man lying on the sand, face down. Will asked, "Who is he?"

"I dunno. Ain't turned him over yet. I was squattin' yonder. This gent staggers in, like he was drunk. I was at the point of hollerin' for him to stop when the guns

73

roared behin' him, an' he fell down on his face."

"Guns?" Will asked. "Out there? Out where?"

"South, behin' him."

"He looks plumb dead," a puncher said. " 'Less I'm cockeyed, he's got three .45 shells in his back. Shot from behin', looks like."

"I never shot him," Wad Jones said. "I ain't packin' no pistol, jus' my Winchester."

"Nobody's accusin' you," Will said.

Will leaned over. He grabbed the man by the shoulders and turned him over. Somebody moved the lantern closer. Will recognized the man instantly. He was as dead as he'd ever be.

"Who is he?" Wad asked.

Will said slowly, "Jennie Clark's father."

Chapter Seven

Jennie Clark had spent a restless night. She was worried about her father. He'd taken the next to last dollar and had walked into town. Fred Bashell—or Mike Amaiz—or somebody had smuggled a bottle to him that afternoon. He weaved as he walked through the *chamisal* and sage.

She had thought of following him, but had hurriedly discarded that plan. When drinking, he was surly and mean. She had seen him once knock her mother down with a single blow when he'd been drunk.

Back east, when drunk he'd invariably gotten into a saloon-brawl. He'd worn black eye after black eye. She'd watched him go with a prayer on her lips and with a hope he'd not get killed.

For in this country men didn't settle differences with fists. They reached decisions by guns or, in the case of the Mexicans, by knives. She then realized he had nobody to argue with.

The other farmers tolerated him. They seemed a close-knit group, for being a bunch of strangers and not meeting the other until they'd settled here on Hatchet graze.

She and her father seemed to be the only newcomers to the group. She didn't know why she just felt that way, but she did. Was Bashell—and Amaiz—settling a bunch of their old friends on Hatchet water?

She was up at dawn, hoeing in her garden. She realized now that Will Cooper had been right—this land would raise nothing but native foliage that for centuries had adapted itself to the chemical structure of Mussampa Basin soil.

Her garden was worthless. Occasionally a few seeds—mostly beans—had sprouted, but they'd soon bent over and now were dry and worthless. She had talked to a Mexican lady in town, whom she'd seen hoeing her garden the other day. the *señora* had given her the same information that Will had given.

"How is it you can raise vegetables and I can't?" she had asked.

The reason was simple. When building Gila City, Abe Cooper had sent wagons to the northern mountains to bring back mountain soil. "He put at least a foot an' one-half on each lot," *Señora* Martinez informed.

"Now I understand," Jennie had said.

"The *Don* Cooper—*el viejo*—was a wonderful man.

76

He knew us *Mejicanos* could not live without plenty of *frijoles* and *tortillas*."

Jennie had known that *tortillas* were dough cakes pounded flat, but *frijoles* was a new Spanish word to her. She'd long ago learned that you acquired knowledge by asking questions, so a question she asked and she discovered *frijoles* were nothing more than beans.

"What kind of a man is the young Mister Cooper?" she asked.

"He is like his good father—kind, considerate, and good to us, *los pobres,* the poor. We all pray he kills every man who tried to steal his water-holes, *los diabbs.*"

"Then he'll have to kill me," Jennie had said, smiling, "for my father and I are homesteading Strawberry Springs.

"Oh, *Dios* forbid!" And portly *Señora* Martinez had made the sign of the cross over her ample bosom.

That long hot night, Jennie went away many times to the front of the dugout and peered east, looking for her father—but dawn finally came and still no Smith Clark.

Worry gnawed her with sharp teeth. She was sure something drastic had happened. With her father, she prepared for the worst and continuously prayed for the rest.

Fred Bashell and Mike Arnaiz rode in at dawn.

"My father—" she said. "What happened?"

" Fred Bashell said, "I have sad news, Jennie. I guess I might just as well break it suddenly, though—for your father is dead!"

Jennie hadn't expected this. She'd figured on a saloon fight or that her father was in the Gila City lockup, but dead—

She said, "He's— He's dead?"

Fred Bashall dismounted but Mike Arnaiz still sat saddle—solid, tough, gun-hung, eyes moving here, then there, always on the alert.

Jennie caught herself. "What happened to him?"

"The Hatchet outfit killed him," Bashell said. "Shot him in the back, when he was on foot on the hill south of Hatchet's house."

Jennie frowned. "How did he come to go to Hatchet? Hatchet's north of town. His homestead is due east."

"He was drunk," Bashell said.

Jennie swallowed. Her throat was bone dry. A cow bawled toward the north, and other cattle began bawling, too.

The bawling came from Cooper Hatchet cows. They stood beyond the barbwire homestead fence. They wanted water.

They'd been there bawling when she'd come into the garden, just as dawn was beginning to peep over the eastern scarp mountains, miles and miles away, but still visible in Arizona's clean air.

They'd leave when the sun got too hot. There must have been water west, for they always went in that direction.

Jennie breathed deeply. Fred Bashell watched her dress rise and fall in front, as she pulled air into her lungs. "Let's go under the tarp in the shade and you tell me all," she said.

"It's a sad, sad tale," Fred Bashell said.

Mike Amaiz now dismounted. He led his bronc and Bashell's toward the dugout. Soon, all three were seated there on boxes, and a ledge that Smith Clark had dug with a spade out of the hillside.

Fred Bashell did the talking.

He told how her father had arrived in town on foot. He'd immediately gone to the saloon. He wanted to fight somebody, but nobody would fight him.

Jennie said, "That's true to form."

He'd drunk until about two in the morning. He'd then run out of money. He'd tried to borrow money. By that time the bar had only the bartender, the swamper, a wandering cowpuncher and Smith Clark.

"He wanted to fight the cowpuncher because the man'd lend him no money," the land-locator said. "The bartender talked him out of that givin' him a pint of Old Horseshoe."

"An' then?"

"This is second-hand, of course—I was sound asleep at that hour. He left and the bartender figured he was headin' home. Well, nobody heard or saw a thing of him, until Hatchet cowpunchers brought in his body early this mornin' in a spring-wagon."

"He'd been shot?"

"Three times," Fred Bashell said and slowly added, " From behin', too."

Jennie tried to gather her thoughts. With a sense of loss was a sense of relief. Her father's drunkeness had been a constant expense to her and her mother, and sometimes she thought her mother had been lucky to die when she had, for by dying she'd got from under the ever-hanging responsibility.

"Why should he be going to Hatchet?" she wondered.

"He was awful drunk, the bartender said. He might've got confused in the dark an' walked the wrong direction, him bein' new to this country."

"Who on Hatchet shot him?"

"That ain't certain," Fred Bashell said. "Hatchet had guards out. The guard on thet side of the ranch house—the south side—said he never fired a shot. The other guard said he was way across the flat on the hill behin' the barn. He never knew a thing about anybody comin' in, until he heard the three shots that kilt your father."

"Was he shot with a rifle or a pistol?"

Fred Bashell looked inquiringly at Mike Arnaiz. "You saw the body this mornin'. What would you say?"

"Looked like rifle holes to me."

Bashell looked at Jennie. "Why did you ask that?"

Jennie had her red head in her hands. She wanted to weep but she couldn't. The sense of relief had overcome the feeling of shock. She was alone in the world now, but she was better off than she'd been since girlhood when she hadn't known about her father's drunkeness.

"I just asked," she said.

Mike Arnaiz said, "I figure that Will Cooper snuck in behin' your dad an' deliberately kilt him from behind, Miss Clark."

"Why Mister Cooper?" Jennie asked.

"The guard claims he never kilt your pappy. Swears up an' down he didn't. Said somebody shot from behin'. Cooper's the kind who'd shoot from the bresh, in my way of thinkin'," Arnaiz said.

Jennie didn't agree with Mike Arnaiz's line of thinking, but she raised no objections. "Where's my father—where's his body now?" she asked.

They had Smith Clark laid out on a house-door on sawhorses in the saloon. Young Doctor Martinez was licensed as the county coroner's assistant for the Gila City area. "He's goin' t' hold an inquest at one. You'd best ride in with us, Miss Jennie."

Jennie agreed she should.

"I'll handle all funeral arrangements," Fred Bashell offered. "I got a hunch how rotten you must feel, Miss Clark."

Mike Arnaiz said, "You know that Pronto Robbins got kilt yesterday in a gunfight in the saloon, didn't you?"

Jennie Clark raised her head. "Pronto Robbins...Oh, yes, he's the farmer who always has his gun tied down to his hip. Who killed him?"

"Will Cooper," Fred Bashell said.

"How'd that happen?"

Fred Bashell did the talking. "Young Cooper an' thet damn' Injun friend of his—thet old man—were drinkin' in the saloon."

Jennie made a mental note. Will Cooper...in the saloon. Maybe he wouldn't be such a good marital partner at that...She'd been plagued her few years by her father's whiskey appetite. She wanted no man who spent more money on booze than on food for the family.

She corrected that: She wanted no man who hung around saloons.

"Then what?" she asked.

"Pronto wanted no trouble with Cooper. He turned and started out to escape trouble, because Cooper had been drinkin' steady. Cooper challenged him and killed Robbins as he was leavin'."

"Won't the law arrest Mister Cooper?"

Fred Bashell laughed sourly. "Hatchet can do anythin' it wants here, an' Cooper is Hatchet. We bury poor Pronto at noon today. Cooper never even offered to go Robbins' funeral expenses. Us farmers'll have to foot that bill. This thing is drawin' to a fine head, Miss Clark."

"What'd you mean by that?"

"Us farmers gotta do one thing—an' that's stick together, all for one and one for all. If we don't, we go under."

Jennie didn't see him wink covertly at Mike Arnaiz, who'd listened with a straight face. Fred Bashell worked on the principle that if you tell a lie, tell a big one. A big one many times is easier to believe than a small one. And what if this pretty little redhead heard different from other lips?

She'd heard him first, hadn't she?

Jennie looked at the Hatchet cattle. A few were trailing over the western hill having given up getting water at Strawberry. "I sure can't handle this homested alone," she said. She almost added that the land was worthless and the only thing of value on the hundred-and-sixty acres was Strawberry Springs. "I wonder if somebody will buy my homestead rights."

"They possibly can be sold," Fred Bashell said.

Again, he winked covertly at Mike Arnaiz. The wink said, she hasn't read the fine print. She doesn't know that if this homestead is sold it can only be bought by one man, and no other—and that man is one Frederick Wagner Bashell.

"I'll have to get to town," she said.

Bashell said, "Mister Arnaiz an' me will harness your team, Miss Clark. Again, I'm sorry we had to be bearers of such sad news."

"Somebody had to tell me," Jennie said.

She went into the dugout to pretty up a bit. The horses loafed in the shade of a big cottonwood by the Springs. They started to run upon seeing their mortal two-legged menace approaching, but Arnaiz ran them down and roped them one by one, busting each hard in the dust.

When the horses regained their hoofs, they were suddenly humble and meek, submitting to harness and bridle and being hitched to the spring-wagon.

Arnaiz said quietly, "Do you think she is as stupid as she acts, or is she tryin' to pull a windy on us?"

"She ain't doin' no bawlin'," Bashell quietly said.

Arnaiz smiled. "What would she have lost to bawl about?" He laughed at his own witticism. "Thet thing she had for a pa should have been still-born."

"Here she comes now," Bashell said.

Jennie wore a plain gingham dress, the skirt gored and flowing. Bashell helped her into the wagon, catching a glimpse of a fine ankle as it passed by his nose.

"I'll lope ahead," Mike Amaiz said.

Fred Bashell turned the team toward Gila City. The day was going to be another scorcher. Already, heat waves danced in the distance.

"We bury your father this afternoon, Miss Jennie," he said. "There are no embalming facilities in Gila City, you know."

Jennie nodded. "I suppose the farmers will all come in to town, seeing both my father and Mister Robbins are being buried?"

"They'll be in. Why did you ask?"

"Well, if Hatchet is in town, too—" She left the rest unsaid.

Fred Bashell slapped the rein against a horsefly feasting on the rump of the nigh horse. "I've thought of that. I'd send Mike out to tell the farmers not to come in, but it's too late. He couldn't reach all the homesteads in time because they're so far apart."

"And all on Hatchet water-holes, too," Jennie said.

Bashell glanced at her. "Why did you say that?"

"Just thinking out loud." Jennie put on her head a big silk handkerchief, one her mother had made for her when she'd been going to Normal school. She began to weep quietly.

Fred Bashell drove on and said nothing for some time. Wheels ground sand and an occasional rock. Shod hoofs lifted, hesitated, then fell. Dust rose from under steel rims. Bashell saw a circle of buzzards off north a few miles. Satisfaction lighted his ruddy face. Probably another dead Hatchet cow? Died from lack of water?

When Hatchet was broke, and the deeds all in his name, he would deliver Mussampa Basin to his New York boss—lock, stock and barrel. The boss wanted to put black Angus on this range. He planned to interbreed Angus and Brahma bulls. The Brahma blood would make the cross-bred Angus tick-proof, for one thing.

The cross-breed would also be a better forager. He'd get fat where a longhorn would remain all bones and hide and horns—and very little meat. He could go longer without water, also.

And the boss would pay plenty. He had a few million dollars he'd made here and there, like cornering the sugar—or coffee—market. And if he didn't pay high in the thousands, he'd not get this water. For the water, when this was finished, would all be in his name—the name of Fred Bashell.

Finally Bashell said, "There's another theory goin' aroun', Miss Jennie, about your father's passing."

"Yes, an' it?"

"Thet him an' Pronto Robbins were good friends. That drunk as your father was, he was mixed-up enough—upstairs, you understan'—thet he suddenly decided to go to Hatchet an' kill the man who had murdered his friend, Pronto."

Jennie considered that. Inside, she was almost laughing despite her recent tragedy.

Her father and Pronto Robbins were not close friends. For one thing, Smith Clark hadn't been on this range long enough to make a tried and true friend.

Two days ago Pronto Robbins had ridden in, gun and loaded cartridge belt and all, with a quart of Old Overshoe. He and her father had killed the quart and as a result, Pronto Robbins has still been on his feet but Smith Clark had lain on the dug-out's dirt floor snoring loudly.

Pronto had then tried to corral Jennie in a corner. Jennie had picked up her butcher knife. Pronto Robbins had pushed in, and Jennie had put the sharp tip against his breast with his hot, stinking whiskey-breath assailing her—and Jennie Clark had pushed.

Not too hard a push, though—not hard enough to cut skin, but to cut a slit in the gunman's shirt and undershirt. Pronto Robbins had jumped back, cursed her, snagged his stirrup and ridden out, gun blasting lead harmlessly into the blue Arizona sky.

Jennie didn't quite understand this land-locator. She had gone to the Wild Rose dance with him last Saturday night just to have somebody to take her there, for her father had been drunk, as usual.

Fred Bashell had tried to put his arm around her while he'd driven her home in the Sunday dawn, but she'd discreetly pushed it aside. Now he was telling her things that she knew possibly could not be true—

Or could they?

Her father had been a drunk. He got crazy ideas from a bottle. He *might* have headed toward Hatchet to try to kill Will Cooper because Will had killed Pronto Robbins.

She had to talk to Will. She'd only met him once, but that single meeting had left a great impression on her. She tried to blame it on loneliness. Had she met Will back east—where there were plenty of other young and good-looking other men—she might have given Will Cooper only a passing glance.

Or would she have?

She glanced down at her sprained ankle. It was almost healed. Will had been a great help that day. What would she have done had he not come riding over that hill?

She'd talk to Will Cooper.

Chapter Eight

Hatchet put Smith Clark's bullet-ridden body on an old door that had been in Hatchet's store room. They placed this—and the body—over two saw-horses in the back of the ranch's spring-wagon.

Anna Cooper watched discreetly from around the heavy window-drape in the living-room. Her son had not told her what had happened. Will had not wanted to waste time explaining, so he'd sent one of the oldest Hatchet cowpunchers, Dick Case, to tell his mother of Smith Clark's death.

Will had given orders that no Hatchet man could go with the funeral wagon into Gila City. He figured the farmers would be there for the double burial of Smith Clark and Pronto Robbins.

Only Apache Ike—and the guard, Wad Jones—would go with him. Jones would ride on the seat and Apache Ike would ride on horseback.

Hatchet cowpunchers—especially the older ones who'd known Abe Cooper well—were against this, and Tom Rutherford said, "There'll be *mucho* farmers there, Will. They'll be drinkin'. It'd be you three ag'in the mob."

Will said, "I understan' how you men feel, Tom, but look at it thisaway. With you boys in town, they's boun' to be trouble. But with only three Hatchet men in town, I doubt if the farmers will all go against three—they've got some sense of fairness, I'd say."

"Maybe, Will, maybe—but them farmers ain't farmers. They're gunmen, Will. Only this Clark idiot wasn't a gunman. How he got in with them farmers I don't know, but I have an idea."

"What is that?

"Smith's daughter, thet purty redhead. Fred Bashell saw her an' got papa to homestead so Bashell could work next to the daughter an' by hoppin' toads, I don't blame him one bit. Were I eighty or so years younger, I'd court her myself, I would!"

Will smiled. "Never knew you were over the hundred mark, Tom. Nope, you boys go about your chores."

"Won't be no chore to string barbwire aroun' the waterin' holes thet ain't already homesteaded, 'cause there's only a coupla them an' them's way out in the hell-an-gone."

Will had to admit that the old rider was right. Fred Bashell and Mike Arnaiz had sneaked in settlers to hold down water before he had been fully aware of what had been going on.

"That may be, Tom, but homestead them as fast as you can."

"What if they've already got sodbusters on 'em?" The old man's eyes lighted. "We light into 'em with Winchesters an' side-arms, an' drive 'em off er kill 'em?"

Will shook his head. "You jus' leave them where they are. You don't bother 'em, understan'?"

"I don't getcha, Will. Your father'd—"

Again, Will shook his head. "Abe Cooper'd not use force. I agree with my father. Black alkali—and drought—will drive them out."

"But they don't aim to settle fer good, Will. They'll deed their water to Bashell, the bastard, an' then he'll own Mussampa Basin because he owns the water. I say ride into town. Meet them gun to gun, an' kill off the sonsofbitches!"

"Tom's right," another old rider said.

Will said, "You boys must be tired of livin'." He picked up the reins and shifted on his high spring seat, Wad Jones sitting beside him. "I'm the boss here, I'm here to say—an' head out with wagons an' barbwire, savvy?"

His voice held finality.

The funeral wagon was clear of the ranch when Wad Jones said, "Why don't you let us wipe out those sodmen, Will?"

"Because they might wipe out more of you boys than you wipe them out," Will said. "Does that make sense?"

"To a point, yes—but there's more than a life at stake. There's Hatchet, itself."

Will nodded. "Yes, but without men—there'd be no Hatchet. Hatchet would be only what it was for centuries and centuries—a desert land only fit for raisin' cattle—or goats—an' then needing around ten acres for each cow."

"There's a thing called pride."

"I agree with that. But right now, in my estimation, pride and property has to be pushed aside, an' let Nature take its course."

"What if Nature doesn't?"

"Then it's guns," Will said.

Wad Jones said, "That's better talk. That's Hatchet talk."

Funerals in Gila City were held in the saloon, the only place in town large enough to hold the mourners. Within a few minutes after arrival, Will knocked on the door of young Doc Martinez who came to open it with a shaving mug in hand and face covered with lather.

Will told of Smith Clark's death.

"I'll be right down to the saloon," the doctor said.

Will entered and closed the door behind him. Doc Martinez returned to his shaving. Will said, "I want the bullets taken out of Clark."

"Why?"

"I want to send them to Tucson. I want to find out what caliber they are. Wad Jones said he packed no short-gun, only a Winchester. I believe him, but I want the leads to make sure."

"No need to send them to Tucson."

Will's brows rose. "Nearest gunshop of any size, Doc."

"I got the table of bullet-weights last week from Winchester's head office back east. Wrote for it. I got gold scales. I can weigh the lead here, just as accurate as they can in Tucson."

"Okay, do that."

"You don't want anybody else to know I took the lead

from Clark, do you?"

"You'll work in private. I'll have a canvas tarp hung from the ceilin' to the floor around the bodies until funeral time."

"Who's going to preach the funerals? This town has no priest. Can't support a *padre*."

"There'll be one sermon for both bodies, an' you'll preach it."

Martinez wiped away the last of the lather. "Suits me fine. Five bucks from Hatchet, mebbeso five from the farmers. Ten bucks is ten bucks, either in Mex or gringo."

"Money talks, friend."

Will left. He moved out into a blistering hot day. He had a sudden terrible thought. Hatchet cattle stood outside of wicked barbwire fences, bawling at fenced-in waterholes.

Maybe the Hatchet men were right? Maybe the only way to solve this problem—to rip down those fences—was with guns, gunsmoke and roaring death?

He remembered he had been about to send out punchers with shovels and picks to dig wells. Things had piled up so fast and so hard he'd momentarily forgotten that.

With Smith Clark dead, would Jennie own rights to the Strawberry Spring homestead?

If so, maybe he could buy her out? Hatchet cattle once again could drink unhindered at Strawberry Springs.

He then remembered Sheriff Dickinson saying that in Nebraska and Wyoming, Fred Bashell had had fine-print clauses in all homestead-entries. If the homesteader sold his homestead rights, he could sell them to one man, and one only—and that man was Fred Bashell.

These local homestead papers would contain the

same clause, Will felt sure. Fred Bashell was smart. He overlooked nothing.

Farmer rigs were arriving. Again Will noticed the hard faces, the pouched guns, of the farmers. They apparently didn't see him as he passed. They busied themselves with tie-ropes and had other chores immediately pop up that required their eyes and their backs be to him.

Will went to the saloon. There, he had Tina and the swamper move the doors holding the two bodies into a corner. Tina didn't have a tarp and he sent the swamper to the *casa* of *Señora* Gonzales to see if she had some old sheets to cover the corner and the corpses.

Señora Gonzales had sheets. She also sent word back for Will Cooper and Hatchet to kill off more farmers.

"She is drunk," she swamper said. "She is full of *vino rojo* an' she is amorous. She tried to drag me into her *recamara*."

"So that's what took you so long," Will said.

"I did not drag. I do not drag easy. I get three beers for runnin' this *chamba*, do I not, *patron* Will?"

Will winked discreetly at Tina. "Only two," he said. "We want you sober for the funeral."

"One should get drunk at funerals. A soul is liberated from trouble an' misery. A man should celebrate at a funeral an' shed tears at birth."

Will remembered Abe Cooper saying that. "Three it is, then," he said. "Here comes Doc Martinez."

Martinez—and black bag—disappeared behind the curtain. Will slipped in with him to make sure nobody else entered. They put Clark Smith on his belly. "Bullets never came out his front," Doc Martinez said. "I'll bet you a *peso* against a *peso* that we find pistol leads in him. A rifle bullet would have gone straight through."

Doc Martinez's scalpel split flesh already tightening into rigor mortis despite the heat. The bullet holes were all under the shoulders, well above the waist.

The holes opened wide enough, pincers were inserted. They probed, found, tightened—then rose; a bloody bullet was in their jaws.

The bullets were soon on a small bit of gauze. Will said, "Those are pistol bullets. Look to me like .45 leads. I'm damn' sure they're .45s doc."

"They look like that to me, too, but my scales will tell."

They took the bullets to Doc Martinez's office. Once again, Will ran the gauntlet of farmers studied indifference.

Will got the feeling that a few of the farmers would have liked to challenge him, but apparently Bashell held them under strict orders. He'd heard that Bashell had given them orders not to move against Hatchet—or a Hatchet man—unless forced.

Will also noticed that some of the farmers were heading for the saloon. And he knew full well the trouble whiskey could start. He wondered if it would not be wise for Wad Jones and old Apache Ike and himself to head back to Hatchet and not attend the funerals.

None of them were interested in the corpses.

Doc Martinez got out his balance scales and his book of bullet weights. The bullets were .45 caliber, as Will had said.

The doctor looked at Will. "I just happened to think, coming down the street, that I can't think of a one of those farmers who is a married man with a wife and family."

"They aren't farmers," Will said. "They're gunmen posin' as sodbusters. They'll soon have most—if not all—of Mussampa's short supply of water. That's what

Bashell wants."

"Then Hatchet will be no more?"

Will said, "Hatchet will stay in Mussampa. When Hatchet falls, I'll be dead. Now, all we have to do is find the .45 that fired these leads an' we have the man who killed Clark from behin'."

"That's an impossibility, Will. About every man on this desert either packs a .45, or has one somewhere in his house."

Will sighed. "How right, doc." He said, *"Adios,* and stepped outside onto the graveled walk. Then it was, that a stern masculine voice cut the heat from his right.

"God damn you, Cooper, turn aroun'!"

Chapter Nine

Will didn't remember going to his knees. He didn't remember reaching, drawing and leveling. But suddenly he was down low to make a smaller target, big .45 centered on a heavy-set gunman he'd heard called Frank Hoffard.

Hoffard had come from behind a wagon. Will got the impression Hoffard had been laying in wait for him.

Now, Hoffard stood wide-legged, staring into the unwavering muzzle of Will Cooper's Colt, hand frozen on his still-holstered gun.

"What's on your mind, Hoffard?"

Surprise lanced across the bearded, ugly face. When Hoffard had called, Hoffard had had the edge. Now, Will had a gun on him, and Hoffard was plainly puzzled—for Hoffard had bragged about being a fast gun.

Townspeople were converging on them. Doc Martinez had come to his office-door. He was directly behind Will. He darted to his right to get out of the way of bullets...if bullets came.

Hoffard was crouched, hand still on his holstered gun.

Will said shortly, "You called me, gunman. What do you want, you water-stealing, low-down bastard?"

Hoffard's wind-cracked lips opened, but no words came. *Señora* Garcia said loudly, "Damn' mountain Lion must've et his damn' tongue."

Others laughed at that. Short, nervous laughs. Behind Hoffard was a clear lane, townspeople hanging well back on either side—for they too were afraid of stray bullets.

Finally Frank Hoffard said, "Don't kill me, Cooper!" His voice was no more than a croak.

Will's pistol was solid against the gunman. Hoffard still had his right hand on his gun. His hand violently shaking. He withdrew it, fingers down, his hand moving cautiously far out.

"You called to me, remember?" Will said.

"I did, Mister Cooper." Hoffard's voice had more strength now. "Jus' as one neighbor to another, sir."

Will got to his boots. "With your hand on your holstered gun? Is that the way neighbor calls to neighbor, where you come from?"

"I forgot," Hoffard said.

Beyond Hoffard, in the street, the Clark spring-wagon at that moment appeared. Jennie Clark and Fred Bashell were on the seat, Bashell holding the reins. Upon seeing Will with his gun on Hoffard, Fred Bashell immediately handed the reins to Jennie.

"Cooper's tryin' to kill another of my farmers," he told Jennie. "Drive on, so if the man shoots you'll be out of range."

Jennie drove on. Bashell walked rapidly in between Hoffard and Will. He said, "Tryin' to kill one of my farmers, eh, Cooper?"

Will Cooper said, "I'll not waste words on such as you. I should let this hammer fall an' send lead through you an' into Hoffard. Next time you send a gun against me, Bashell, be sure its faster than this clumsy, would-be farmer."

Bashell spoke to Hoffard. "You pull your gun against Cooper?"

Hoffard shook his head. "I jus' called out friendly to him. He went to one knee and first thing I knew, his gun was pointin' at me. I thought for a spell there he'd kill me, sure."

Without warning, five or six or more yards of gingham exploded from the doorway of the Mercantile, and *Señora* Gonzalez arrived on the scene, her protruding front almost colliding with Fred Bashell's middle shirt buttons.

"I saw it all," she said angrily. "This man here—your man, Bashell—tried to kill my friend, Mister Cooper!"

Bashell said, "Apparently there were no shots fired, so how could he have tried to kill Cooper?"

"He didn't have a chance to fire," the busty *señora* said flatly. "My friend—*mi amigo*— was far ahead of him.

Had not my friend been a controlled man, he would have shot your farmer—and killed him in his tracks."

"*Señora* Gonzalez is right, *Señor* Bashell."

Señora Garcia had joined the group. Fred Bashell looked at a loss. He faced at least four hundred pounds of unpleasant, dark-skinned flesh. This was definitely a thing he'd not anticipated.

Will Cooper pouched his .45. He looked upstreet. Jennie had pulled the old nags to a halt in front of the hardware store's hitchrack. She came down and began tying them to the rack with their halter ropes.

Will admired her small waist. He was at the point of going in Jennie's direction when a man said, "Your mama, Will. Across the street."

Startled, Will shot a glance across the dust. His mother's red-wheeled buggy had just rolled around the corner—or had it? He spoke to the man. "How long has she been there?"

"Quite a while. She sat an' watched."

"Did she see me pull my gun on this dog-farmer?"

"She came at that moment."

Will pulled air into his lungs. He hurriedly thought back and came to the conclusion his mother had not been in Gila City—or off the ranch—for at least a year. Now what had brought her into town?

"She could have stopped lead," Will said.

"I doubt that. She's upstreet too much."

Will looked across the gathering at his mother. She sat prim and slender, with a parasol over her head and the hand holding the parasol handle wore a thin laced white glove. Will remembered his father bringing the red parasol and the gloves back from Los Angeles as a present.

Abe Cooper had gone to Los Angeles with a trainload of Hatchet steers loaded out of Tuscan.

The Cocopah squaw drove the team. Squaw was bareheaded and her gray hair was in two braids down the front of her old gingham dress.

Anna Cooper stared straight ahead. She had no eyes for the group around Bashell and Hoffard. She apparently had no interest in anything.

Will stepped off the graveled walk to begin to cross the street to his mother.

His mother said, "Drive on, Virginia."

The squaw drove on. Will looked at Hoffard. Will said, "You sonofabitchin' gundog playin' as a farmer!"

Hoffard hit. Will went under. Hoffard's fist missed. The miss brought Hoffard lurching ahead—into Will Cooper's right uppercut.

Later, onlookers said the blow lifted the heavy farmer off the ground. Will didn't know. He didn't care. He had to hit something. Hoffard had been the closest.

And he'd had a reason for hitting the farmer.

Hoffard staggered back. Will hit him flush in the face three more times. Hoffard went against the rear wheel of his rig. He was out in his boots. He wanted to fall, but Will's blows kept him upright. Finally Will stepped back, and Howard fell.

Will slipped the man's gun from leather. He threw it out into the street dust. He looked at Fred Bashell, who was surrounded by irate townspeople.

"You got anythin' to say, Bashell?"

Bashell looked at Hoffard. Hoffard's face was blood and dust. He looked back at Will Cooper. This had happened so fast he again was at a loss. Finally he said, "I got no quarrel with you, Cooper."

"The way you're goin', you soon will have."

Will then became aware of a feminine hand pulling his arm. He looked down on the red head of little Jennie Clark.

Jennie said quietly, "Will, please..."

Will breathed deeply. He'd made up his mind to kill Bashell, here and now, or to be killed by the land-locator. Jennie's arrival threw water over that plan.

He looked in the direction his mother's buggy had taken. The buggy had stopped in the act of turning the corner.

Squaw looked back but Anna Cooper didn't. Anna Cooper held the red parasol and her back was rigid. You could see that, even at that distance.

Then, Squaw turned. Will got the impression his mother had spoken to Squaw. The rig moved out of sight around the corner.

Jennie's small hand gently pulled. "Will, please come. It will only be another death—or two—And one could be yours." Her voice held tears. She had not wept at her drunken father's death but she was close to it now, and at that moment she couldn't have explained why. "Come with me, Will."

Will said, "This is only the second time we've met."

He didn't know why he'd said that, but he had. They walked away, her hand on his elbow.

He said, "Your poor father—"

"Yes."

"Wad Jones didn't kill him. Wad had a rifle. I checked the barrel. It hadn't been fired recently. Wad swears up and down he never fired a shot. He said he'd put his hand on the Bible and swear."

"Wad Jones?"

"The guard we'd stationed. I've known him almost all my life. He came to the ranch as a stray kid. My dad took a fancy to him. He'd never lie to me nor me to him, Jennie."

"Then who did kill my father?"

"I don't know who killed him," Will said, "but I do

know why. Somebody wanted to lay the blame of his death on Hatchet."

"Why?"

"To get the farmers—if you can call them that—into a fightin' mood, so mebbeso they'd even tackle Hatchet on its home grounds."

"Who would gain by that?"

" Fred Bashell."

"You mean that Bashell wants your ranch?"

"He certainly does. I don't think he wants it for himself. He wants it for a third party, somebody with money who's hired him to steal Hatchet's water-holes. For without water I'll have to jus' let my cattle die of thirst or ship every head out."

"Your poor cows were on the other side of my fence this morning, bawling for water. It hurt me. My heart went out to them. I never knew they'd have no water if we fenced Strawberry Springs."

"How did your father get mixed in with a rat like Bashell?" Will asked.

"Jus' by accident. We decided to go west. Dad got fired from the police force of our home town—back east—because of his drinking. So we went west. We stopped for a day or so in Tucson. Dad met Bashell in the usual place he met people—a saloon."

Will listened. His nerves were settling down. His right knuckles were skinned. Will looked back. Bashell had Hoffard on his feet. Hoffard leaned against the wagon's hind wheel, sleeving blood from his nose. The crowd was breaking up and heading for the saloon— men and women and children—to view the remains of Smith Clark and Pronto Robbins.

"Dad told me all about the meeting. He says that Bashell just showed interest in him when Dad mentioned that when he'd been on the police force, he had gold cups and ribbons and such things for his marksmanship.''

"With a rifle? Or a pistol?''

"With both. He holds the state police record for drawing and firing a pistol, and hitting his target six shots out of six—and every shot through the target's heart, or close to it.''

Will now understood. Fred Bashell had actually hired Clark because of his ability with a gun. He evidently hadn't banked on Smith Clark being drunk all the time—or close to it.

"Did you ever notice that none of the other homesteaders have women?'' Will said.

"I understand three had, but the women immediately left. I've heard they were—well, let's be generous and call them *dance-hall girls*.''

"I didn't know that,'' Will said. "What are you goin' to do with your homestead? Stay out the two years until you get final papers?''

"How can I? What will I eat on?   Jackrabbits?''

"You can teach school here in Gila City. Our teacher quit this spring. I'm head of the schoolboard. I'll see you get the job.''

"Who told you I was a school teacher?''

Will smiled. "I knew that the minute you tied into me for nothin' the other day. All school teachers, I've heard, get bossy—and right off the bat you started bossin' me aroun'.''

Jennied looked at him. "Will, am I really that bossy?''

"You were that day.''

"That was a bad, bad day. Everything went wrong. You're joking with me, aren't you?''

Will had begun to feel uncomfortable. His tongue had worked him into a corner. His day had not been a good one, either. He'd little sleep last night. His mother had bawled him out in another endless argument, pointless and vacillating. Then Smith Clark had been murdered.

Jennie's question gave him an out. He said, "I was jus' jokin', Jennie. You could still homestead an' teach."

"I want to get rid of the Springs. I want your cattle to have water. I don't want to torture innocent animals. Will you offer me a fair price for it?"

Will shook his head.

"I thought you wanted the Springs?"

"I do, but you can't sell it," Will pointed out.

"Why can't I?"

Will said, "I don't know if it's true or not, but I've heard from reliable sources that the fine print in the contracts you settlers have with Fred Bashell says you can sell to only one person— Fred Bashell."

"Is that true?"

Will shrugged. "So I've heard."

"We'll settle that, here and now," Jennie said. "I have the contract in my purse. Where can we go and read it carefully?"

"In the saloon."

"Saloon? Why, I've never been in a saloon in my life, not even to get my father—and I'm not going in now. Do you drink much?"

Her blue eyes studied his face, noticing the effects of the fight at her homestead were fading away—although a light blue ring still hung like a half-halo under his right eye.

"Jus' a beer now an' then, an' it's more than now. But there's an office there—off to one side—We can slip in by the back door, if you like—and then we won't have to go through the saloon itself."

Will looked back as they disappeared around the west corner of the saloon. People watched. Will said, "They think I'm takin' you into the brush, Jennie."

"What would be wrong with—Will Cooper, what am I saying? I talk to you as though you and I were reared together since we were children—why do I like you, Will?"

"Mebbeso it's because I'm the papa of around eighteen to twenty thousan' head of bony longhorn cattle, who right now are in a race to see whether they die for lack of pasture or lack of water."

"Will, I'm turning around, right now, and leaving you."

Will shook his head. He took her firmly by an elbow. She had a nice elbow, he discovered. "I'm sorry, Jennie. No, I'm not sorry. I'm jus' happy I met you once again, that's all."

"You're pushing me, Will!"

"I can push harder, Jennie."

They arrived at the office door. Will pulled on the latchcord and the door opened to expose a dust-covered desk and chairs. "Last used by my father," Will said. "I don't have much to do with the saloon, even though Hatchet owns it. Tina keeps books and records and gives me the cash when we get a surplus."

"Tina? Your girl-friend?"

"Bartender, male. Tina means Tub in Mexican, and a tub of guts he is." Will brushed dust from a chair with his Stetson. "Sit down, please, Jennie."

Jennie produced the contract. Will read it and discovered the clause saying a homesteader—the signer—could sell only to Fred Bashell. He pointed it out to Jennie, who read faster than he.

Jennie put the legal-looking paper down and said, "Well, I'll be hornswoggled. That dirty—" She paused.

"I can see nothing that forbids me from cutting the fence and letting your poor cows drink."

Will slowly shook his head. "Don't do it, Jennie."

"Why not? Your cows—they're suffering—?"

"You'll be livin' alone. You might suddenly disappear. And I'll bet the wires would go right up again, without you aroun'."

"Disappear? Where to? And why?"

"Unless I'm wrong, Bashell has a few thousand—and quite a few—coming to him if this scheme to steal Mussampa from Hatchet works. And Bashell will allow no person, dead or alive, to stand between him an' that money, if I see it correct."

"You mean he'd—well, do away with me?"

"I wouldn't put it beyond him."

Jennie frowned prettily. "I can hardly believe that. This is Arizona—and Arizona is not civilized enough yet to become a state, but still—A woman, alone?..."

"Don't bet too much," Will said.

"I'll think it over, Will. That lady in the buggy—out on mainstreet a while ago—Sitting so stately and regal with the red parasol. Somebody said that was your mother."

"That was Anna Cooper," Will assured.

"Anna? Your father had a sister, a female Cooper, named Anna?"

Will said dryly, "Anna Cooper is my mother. Most people—well, I always think of her as Anna, not as mother. Or mama. Even when I was a child, I had a hard time calling her mama. I wanted to call her Anna."

"Didn't she ever pick you up—rock you to sleep— When you were little, of course?"

"If she did, it was before I started rememberin' things." Will got to his feet. "She's—Well, how will I put it?" He thought for a moment, her blue eyes on him. "I'll say it this way—I believe she hasn't all her right senses."

Jennie stood up. She watched his face, but had no words.

"She's never been real," Will said. He added, "To me, at least. She's always lived where others didn't live, if you understand what I mean?"

"I do. I had a few girls like that in my classes. I'd talk to them and they'd nod and give the right answers, but their minds and imaginations were thousands of miles away."

"That's how it is with Anna Cooper. My father—He finally left the house. He ate with the crew in the chuck-shack. He slept in the foreman's shack, after putting the foreman in the bunk-house."

"And you?"

"All my life—since I can remember—I slept in the bunkhouse an' ate with the Hatchet men in the chuck-shack. I don't know why. It seemed like the proper thing to do at that time."

"And your mother has lived alone all these years?"

Will said, "I can't build the bridge. I start and her words tear out the pilin's, or a blunder of my tongue ruins it all. You can thank yourself for one thing, Jennie—your father might have drunk, but I think you an' him had something between you—the love a man should have for his daughter, and the daughter for her father."

Tears filled her blue eyes. "I thank you for that, Will Cooper. Yes, dad and I might have had our bad moments, but nothing could have parted us but death—which death finally did."

"What would you do if you discovered who murdered your father?"

"I would do nothing to them. That night in my

105

prayer before bed, I'd ask God to forgive them, for they are only stupid mortals, too."

Will studied her. She meant every word. At that moment the big bald head of Tina appeared at the single window. He tapped and said, " Funeral about ready to start, boss."

Will dug out his dollar Ingersoll. "Ahead of time, ain't you, Tina?"

"Terribly hot day, Will. Meat don't keep long in weather like this." Tina's head disappeared.

Chapter Ten

Fred Bashell and Mike Amaiz did not sit with the other mourners on the wooden benches the town carpenter had built years ago, for dances and funerals and other public events.

The two stood at the bar, each with a bottle of Tucson beer. Across the saloon, Will Cooper and Apache Ike sat on a bench placed against the wall. Jennie Cooper sat between them.

This fact didn't please Fred Bashell. He had his own plans for Jennie Cooper and they did not include matrimony. Only a fool would get married and raise a bunch of snot-nosed, sassy kids. Life had enough complications without a man going out and deliberately seeking more.

A year from now, he told himself, there'd be another Jennie somewhere, only god knew where—but there'd be one. There always had been one. There always would be, he figured, until he got so damn' old the females wouldn't look at him—the pretty young ones, that was.

Yet it looked like young Cooper, without even doing any visible work in that direction, had cut him out—and he had a hunch this whole gossipy town had an idea he was making a play for redhead Jennie Clark.

This small town was no different than all small towns. Everybody knew the past and present of everybody else and, because they knew each other and lived together in a congested area, they naturally envied the other—and envy, he knew, was the foundation of hate.

They smiled and appeared friends on the streets or at gatherings, but deep inside they forced themselves to tolerate the other. And they had eyes that saw everything and ears that heard everything and what they didn't see or hear they imagined, and none of their imaginings were complimentary, one reason so many lived in big cities.

It angered him to see Jennie sitting with Hatchet. Hadn't she a bit of pride? Or common sense? Hadn't her father been killed but a few hours before, on Hatchet property?

Evidently she didn't think Hatchet had murdered her father. If she had, would she be openly and boldly sitting with Hatchet's owner? A touch of jealousy struck him.

Plainly, she and Will Cooper had progressed further than he'd thought. She'd ridden into town with him.

She'd promptly deserted him for Cooper. His pride was hurt.

He'd show that little redheaded bitch! Let her try to sell her homestead entry to Cooper and see how far she'd get!

He knew she now owned all homestead rights on Strawberry Springs. He knew by heart all the stipulations each homestead entry carried.

Fred Bashell lifted his beer bottle. He glanced at glowering, ever-frowning Mike Arnaiz. He wondered if Arnaiz could match Cooper's gunspeed. He'd heard that Abe Cooper and Apache Ike had given Will Cooper many lessons in draw, level and fire.

He'd heard about the shooting matches young Cooper had won at the six-month Hatchet *rodeos*. He'd not tangle with Cooper—with a gun—unless forced. His tongue touched his bottom lip gingerly. Nor in fisticuffs, either.

Cooper's fists had split the inside of that lip. He'd had plenty of Cooper's iron-knuckled fists. He wanted no more. Cooper had been the only man he'd fought with who had cold-cocked him. And Cooper had knocked him into dreamland with just a few blows.

He remembered Cooper's fists hammering down Frank Hoffard. Hoffard had bragged about his prowess as a rough and tumble fighter, too. His thoughts went back to Jennie Clark.

If she cut Strawberry Springs' fence to let Hatchet cattle in to water, Miss Jennie Clark would suddenly disappear. There'd be a note on her table, saying she'd walked to the stage road and caught the Concord running between Nogales and Tucson.

Nobody—not even a pretty young female—was standing between him and around fifty-thousand dollars, U.S. Now he leaned close and said to Mike Arnaiz,

"See Cooper over there?"

"Could I miss seein' him. He's not stealin' your woman. He's already done stole her."

Fred Bashell overlooked that. "Dead, he's worth five hundred cold U.S. bucks, Mike."

Mike Arnaiz said, also in a mere whisper, "You don't touch me, Fred. I've seen that gink handle that cutter. From the bresh, yes—but not in the open, me ag'in him."

"You'd want more?"

"Not a bit more, boss. You couldn't buy me to match him. I know my limits, an' I hope I've seen his—an' we'd be neck an' neck on the far turn, but his turn might be a mite faster'n mine."

"You ascairt of 'im?"

"Not a bit, Fred. I'm only ascairt of two people—an' maybe they ain't people but forces—an' they're the Devil an' God, an' I got more fear of God than the Devil. The Devil an' me—if they is a Devil—seem to be about on the same level."

"Either way," Fred Bashell said, "the money is good—from the night, the day, the front, side or back; jus' so it's done."

"I'll sleep on it. You tol' that to Hoffard, too, didn't you?"

Fred Bashell nodded.

"I've hit with my fists an' clubs an' my gun, but I don't believe I ever seen a man hit so fast, an' so often, in such a short time, as I saw when Cooper's fists hung Hoffard over the line to dry," Arnaiz said.

Fred Bashell's tongue gingerly explored a cut in his bottom lip's inside. "He was even faster'n the other day, looked to me. He's improvin', Mike, with age, mebbeso?"

"Like Swiss cheese," Arnaiz said.

110

They were talking of roaring guns and death, but they might just as well been merely passing the time of day. Each had a face completely without expression and both looked to be merely lounging against the bar, one elbow on the bar and a boot on the brass footrail.

"Another beer?" Bashell asked.

"I could stan' another. Damn' hot day. You spring this time, or is it my turn?"

"Your turn. I bought the last."

Mike Arnaiz dug out a hand-embossed wallet and pulled out four bits. Tina saw the money and came down the line with two cold bottles he'd picked out of the well-bucket as he passed.

Tina uncorked.

Arnaiz said, "Change is yours, *amigo*."

"Thanks," Tina said. "Help buy *huaraches* for my six kids."

"I thought you had nine the last trip down?" Fred Bashell said.

Tina grinned. "Bad memory," he said. "an' it gets worse as I get older." He appeared uncomfortable. He was. He picked up the fifty-cent piece and returned to the bar's end.

Fred Bashell and Mike Arnaiz were the only ones at the bar. They were the only ones drinking. Others wanted to wet their whistles, but did not because of reverance and respect for the two dead men.

"By hell," Fred Bashell said, "Look who's comin', frien'. The queen of Mussampa Basin herself."

Will Cooper's mother was entering. She walked in black, regal, thin and queenly, with Squaw dressed in flaming red, following, her lady in attendance. All eyes turned. To Fred Bashell's surprise, every man, woman and child stood up, even Will Cooper.

Bashell instantly noticed Apache Ike had gone. He

hadn't seen the old Indian slip out, either.

"I don't understan' this," Fred Bashell said. "When she paraded into town in her buggy, she was dressed all in white. Now she's black as sin an' midnight."

"Prob'ly had some black clothes with her."

"Where'd she change, I wonder?"

"Mebbeso out in the high brush," Mike Arnaiz said.

Bashell said, "I wouldn't care to see thet ol' vulture change clothes, but it sure would please me to see Jennie change."

"There's a slight difference in their ages," Arnaiz said. "Jennie might look even worse at the Queen's age."

"Impossible," Bashell said.

Two townsmen hurriedly left the mourner's benches, went back and squatted at the end of the bench holding Jennie and Will, who had now sat down. Anna Cooper sat between *Señora* Gonzalez and old Mateo Cortinez.

Squaw sat on the floor at the end of the bench where Anna Cooper sat. Young Doctor Martinez opened the sermon with a short prayer. He then explained that the killer—or killers—of Smith Clark were still unknown and at large. As a representative of the county coroner for this district, he'd have to make this fact known to the county sheriff.

"Hope they ain't never found," Arnaiz said quietly. "They should get medals for killin' the drunk."

"They won't ever be found," Fred Bashell said.

Arnaiz said, "Why the huge jump from fifty bucks to five hundred, boss. You only paid Pronto fifty, remember?"

"An' like a damn' idiot, I paid ahead of time. Never again in advance. Now, the school or somethin' in town gets the money."

"Five hundred's a lot of dough."

"It's worth it."

Mike Arnaiz listened to Doctor Martinez. The young medico was really getting wound up. After a while Arnaiz said, "Who the hell's he got on them slabs, anyway?"

"Robbins an' Clark, of course."

"Cain't be them. I knew them two bastards purty well, an' what he's saying don't fit them two at all. They won't get no wings when an' if they get through them Pearly Gates. They apparently had wings while here on earth, accordin' to that young Mexican."

"He's gettin' so wound up he's talkin' more Spanish than English," Fred Bashell said. "He's throwin' out sentences that start in English, then change to spic, then back to English ag'in."

"Hell, the ol' Injun—He's gone, Fred."

"You jus' miss him?"

"Hell, he was settin' there jus' a minute ago."

Fred Bashell shook his head. "Quite a few minutes ago. He was gone when Missus Cooper come in."

"You see him go?"

"He slipped out past my eyes, too."

"Jus' like a sneakin' Injun," Arnaiz said. "They're worse than a Mex when it comes to sneakin' in behin' a man's back. They like to use a knife, too— 'cause a knife makes no noise."

"I've met quite a few whites that would do the same," Fred Bashell said. "Wonder where he went, an' why he left?"

"Want me to slip out an' trail him?"

Fred Bashell shook his head. "You an' me are peaceful, law-lovin' citizens, an' two of our friends—dear an' close friends—are being planted—pardon me, I mean buried—and its our obligation to help put them to their eternal rest, and to hell with the Injun."

Mike Arnaiz looked at Fred Bashell. "You been dishin' out the peyote ag'in—an' not to a gink like Pronto Robbins now?"

"You know I never touch it." Fred Bashell's voice held hardness. "Why ask such a nutty question."

"That sentence you jes' said was the longest I believe you ever said in all the time we've sided each other—an how many years has thet been?"

"To damn' many," Bashell said.

Mike Arnaiz knew he had said too much. He'd advanced too far upon his boss's personality. Bashell was like that—he led a man on, let the man break familiarity, then cut him off immediately. And, once again, Mike Arnaiz and Fred Bashell were not friends but one was the hired gun, the other the man who had done the hiring.

Mike Arnaiz, restored to his social niche, found himself looking over the farmers, who sat in a body in the first row of benches. Those that had worked with Fred Bashell on the Belle Fourche River—and even who had helped on Nebraska's Elkhorn—had, of course, changed their names for this job; for Uncle Sam checked names in Washington, D.C., it was said, to make sure no one person filed for two different homesteads when the law allowed him only one filing.

He went from man to man, trying to correctly call to mind their new names. It was quite a job. His memory didn't like to store such things, important as they were.

He came to Fritz Harding, alias Frank Hoffard. To his surprise, Hoffard was now missing, and a few minutes before he'd been sitting with Max Hanson on one side and Herb Fillmore on the other.

But Frank Hoffard was there, no longer.

Mike Arnaiz was on the point of mentioning Hoffard's disappearance to Fred Bashell, and then he thought otherwise. If Bashell was so damned smart, he'd have already noticed Hoffard's absence.

Amaiz needed another beer. The day was a hell-scorcher. He glanced at Bashell's bottle. Bashell had over half left. Amaiz lifted his hand and nodded at Tina.

Thoughtful Tina had pulled up a few buckets of beer from the well before the services had begun. The windlass made a loud squeaking sound as its axles rubbed on the wooden frame, so he had lifted cold beer up and put it under the bar beneath a damp old horse blanket.

He took a bottle from under its damp covering. It was cool and already smelled of horse manure and horse sweat from the blanket. He uncorked it and silently carried it down to Amaiz who lay two-bits on the bar.

Tina pointed suggestively at Bashell's bottle. Bashell was looking at Jennie Clark's knees and didn't see the gesture. Amaiz shook his head and Tina waddled back to his resting place, empty bottle in hand.

Tina put a big paw in the cigar box where he kept change. Mike Amaiz shook his head. Tina put a coin to his lips, kissed it, put it in his apron pocket, and returned to his listening.

Mike Amaiz raised his bottle. Cold beer streaked down his throat. He killed half the bottle at one time. He was lowering the bottle when Fred Bashell said, "You're behin' me, friend."

Bashell hadn't seen him get a new bottle.

"I'll catch up," Amaiz said. "Cripes, ain't this croaker ever gonna run down. He's took off his coat, then his vest, his shirt is wet with sweat, everybody's gettin' thirsty—an' the Queen of Mussampa Basin sits there, lookin' straight ahead, not movin', nothin'."

"I think she's slipped her picket-pin. You see her eyes when she come in? Looked like the eyes of a glass-eyed bronc. Wild an' wooly but no fleas. Hell, he finally got them two stiffs into heaven. He's finally done!"

"He ain't done yet," Mike Arnaiz said. "The bastard's startin' to pray." He grinned at Fred Bashell. "Gonna close your eyes?"

"Why not? Give my eyes a rest. They're full of sand from all this wind." He put his head down.

"Not me," Arnaiz said. "There's too many guns aroun' for comfort."

"Keep guard for me," Bashell said.

The prayer droned on and on. Finally it, too, ended. All stood up. Now was the time to take a last look at the corpses.

Mike Arnaiz said, "Gonna give the stiffs a look, boss?"

Bashell shook his head. "Made me half-sick to look at 'em when they was breathin'. Makes me whole-sick to look at them now they ain't."

"What are they waitin' for?"

"Missus Cooper. She's the dueña, the boss. She should head the procession."

Anna Cooper moved on wooden legs. When she passed the bodies she distinctly said, "Good riddance to bad rubbish."

Fred Bashell grinned. The Hatchet woman moved outside, Squaw dutifully trailing. Bashell and Arnaiz remained at the bar. Most of the men after looking at the bodies hurried to the bar. Tina was busy. The swamper pitched in to help Tina.

Bashell noticed that Will Cooper never looked at the bodies. While Jennie went to see her father for the last time, Will stepped outside. Then it was that smashing gunfire tore through the heat.

All inside stiffened, listening. Bashell went to the door. Will Cooper stood on the stone sidewalk, gun in hand—but Will was not firing. He'd not done the

116

shooting.

Upstreet, old Apache Ike was prone in the dust, long-barreled Peacemaker lying across his forearm, the gun trailing smoke. Bashell looked across the street.

Here was a wooden water barrel placed, in case of fire. Water spurted from a hole close to its bottom. Gunfire came from behind the barrel. Bashell saw dust spout in front of the old Hatchet rider.

Old Apache Ike shot again. Another hole appeared in the bottom of the barrel. The Apache was shooting through the barrel to hit whoever was behind it.

That Hatchet bullet brought the man from his hiding place. Bashell recognized Frank Hoffard immediatly.

Hoffard said, "Don't shoot no more!"

Apache Ike raised his smoking six-shooter. He carefully and slowly got up from the dust.

Frank Hoffard staggered ahead. He dropped his smoking six-shooter. He lurched, then fell on his side. He rolled over on his back. Blood came from his right shoulder.

Old Apache Ike looked at Will Cooper. "You were right when you saw him sneak out on hands an' knees, figgerin' nobody'd see him leave. And I guessed right when I said I'd sneak out after him. He laid an ambush for you, Will!"

Will Cooper said, "Did you get hit?"

Apache Ike shook his head. Anna Cooper walked past the fallen Hoffard. She kicked dust in Hoffard's face.

"More worthless rubbish," she said.

She walked to her buggy.

Chapter Eleven

Next morning, Will Cooper and Apache Ike rode to Cabeza Springs where Will had three men digging a well on the east limit of Frank Hoffard's homestead.

Frank Hoffard's homestead shack consisted of rough planks nailed to posts driven into the ground. The roof was made of *tules* cut from around the spring and laid flat between stringers.

Will had two men digging. The third man kept watch. He now came out of the brush along a hill with his Winchester.

"Everythin' goin' all right?" Will asked.

"All okay, boss."

Will jabbed a thumb toward the shack. "Anybody move in it yet?"

"Guy rode in this mornin'. You can't see his hoss— it's tied behind the shack."

"Know him?" Will asked.

"Never seen him aroun' here before or anywhere else. Where the hell do you suppose the damn' Bashell gets all these guns?"

"Prob'ly got a standin' order for guns in the red-light district in Tucson," Apache Ike said. "Gink ain't said nothin' about you boys diggin' here, I take it?"

"We ain't on his property," the cowpuncher pointed out, "an' if he did, I'd salt him down like you did that Hoffard gink yesterday, Apache. I don't know about you boys, but I'm gettin' kinda tired of bein' pushed aroun'."

Will looked at him. "You're still alive," he said.

"Why'd you say that?" the puncher asked.

"If Hatchet moved against these gunmen, you might be dead. A bullet doesn't give a damn who it hits an' kills," Will said.

"Too bad Apache here didn't kill Hoffard. We'd be minus one enemy."

Frank Hoffard was bedded-down in *Señora* Gonzalez's mud shack. Missus Gonzalez's place acted as a hospital for Doc Martinez's patients. Doc said he'd be around in a day or so, but would have to keep his right arm in a sling.

Apache Ike's bullet had broken Hoffard's right collar-bone.

"I shot to kill the bastard," Apache Ike said, "but I ain't the shot I used to be. Eyes ain't as good. Ten years ago I'd have beheaded him with one slug, an open shot

119

like I had.

"Open shot?" Will asked. "He was hidin' behin' a barrel *amigo*. You call thet an open shot?"

"I sure do. All I had to do was judge which part of the barrel hid him. I figured he'd be crouched or lyin' down, so I shot low on the barrel an' druv him into the clearin'."

They rode downslope to where the two cowpunchers were digging. They'd started yesterday morning and had a good-sized hole six feet deep. They were covered with white alkali mud.

Will and Apache Ike dismounted and walked to the hole. Water had come within six inches of the top. It looked clear and inviting. Will knelt and scooped up a handful and tasted it.

He immediately spit it out. "Alkali an' more alkali," he said. "An' where the spring comes outa rock the water is sweet."

"That's 'cause it comes outa granite," Apache Ike explained, "an' granite can't hol' alkali, I done read in a book Uncle Sam put out—about irrigation, an' things like that."

"Didn't know you could read," Will said, jokingly.

"*Señora* Gonzalez learned me," Apache Ike said, and added, "In bed, of course."

"Of course," Will said. He spoke to the two cowpunchers. "Run a little ditch from the spring downhill an' we'll see if the cows'll drink it.

The shovels rose, fell. Will looked at the hundred or so head of Hatchet cows trying to get to Cabeza Springs. The barbwire fence—five strands—held them back.

The fence was sturdily built with heavy cedar posts. The wires were strung tight and stapled downward. The wire's barbs stuck out ready to tear hide and flesh, be it human or bovine.

Will noticed a few of the cows were wire-cut. They were so thirsty they'd tried getting through the fence. The two bottom wires were close together. This kept the small calves from sneaking in.

But the calves had milk from their mothers. And they'd have no milk unless the cows got water soon.

Water soon trickled down-hill through the makeshift ditch. Will turned some cows in that direction. They tried the water but wouldn't drink. One cow that tried the most, suddenly began to heave. The alkali hit her immediately. She lifted her tail and a stream shot out.

"Powerful stuff," old Apache Ike said.

Will breathed deeply. This seepage-gather idea was no good. He'd not banked much on it, though. It had been the last resort. No, not the last, he corrected—maybe next to the last.

The last resort was gunpowder.

"Why not cut the fence?" a cowboy said. "I got wire-cutters on my saddle, Will."

Will shook his head. "Unless I'm plumb wrong, right now hid in that shack yonder pokes out a Winchester thet has covered us all this time. An' you make a move to cut thet barbwire an' thet rifle'll talk—an' it has the legal right to kill, too."

"I got a rifle. It can talk, too."

"But thet guy in thet cabin might shoot first," Will said. "Tie your shovels onto your saddles an' chouse these cows to the nearest water-hole." He thought for a moment. "Where is there an open water-hole?"

"Magpie Springs," a puncher said. "That's at least twenty miles east." He looked at a cow. "Most might make it in this heat but thet cow there—she'd never be able to navigate it, Will."

He and Apache Ike rode some fifty miles that day checking on well-digging crews. He was surprised to find that one well had sweet water. The water didn't run through sand, but trickled out a ledge of granite.

And it trickled out very, very slowly. Apache Ike figured it ran about a fifty-five gallon barrel in an hour. The water immediately disappeared as bone-showing cows sucked it up, mud and all, other Hatchet cattle crowding behind, bawling and with flanks flat from lack of water.

Apache Ike looked at the sky. There wasn't a cloud in sight, not over the distant mountains. "Does it ever change?"

"Seems like it don't want to," Will said.

Apache Ike looked at his young boss. " For a young stiff, you're one of the most patient men I've ever seen."

"I guess I take after Abe Cooper. I wonder what Abe'd done in a situation like this."

"Jus' about like his son is doin'. He'd take it so long and work for peace, but when he saw it was no use then all hell'd bust loose."

"I wish I knew what to do."

Apache Ike had no answer.

Will turned on stirrups. "What do you say, *amigo?* How do you think it will end? What's the verdict?"

"It'll either end peacefully, or in gunsmoke."

Will laughed shortly. "Why don't you run for public office? Well, down yonder is Strawberry—an' it's got Hatchet cows aroun' its fence, too."

The Clark dug-out was below. Two men on horseback talked to Jennie. A young woman stood beside Jennie.

Apache Ike said, "Bashell an' Arnaiz on their cayuses. Who's the girl with Jennie?"

"Beta Gonzalez. Jennie said Beta would come out and stay with her."

"That's Missus Gonzalez' middle girl, ain't it?"

"Not middle, the youngest."

"She that big already...Time sure flies. First thing I know, I'll be an old man. We ridin' down, or ain't we?"

"We're ridin' down," Will said.

They met Bashell and Arnaiz as the pair rode through the barbwire gate. Arnaiz was on the ground ready to close the gate again and Will said, "Don't mind. We'll close it."

Arnaiz paid no attention. He closed the gate without a word and mounted. Fred Bashell sat a lazy saddle and watched Arnaiz insult the Hatchet men.

Will's face darkened. He rode close to Arnaiz. Their horses stood shoulder to shoulder. Will's face was a few feet from Arnaiz's dark, sardonic features. Will said, "You got ears, you bastard. Why don't you use them?"

Arnaiz said quietly, "The boss says no trouble, Cooper." He looked beyond Will at Fred Bashell. "Or have you changed your orders, boss?"

Apache Ike watched Fred Bashell. Bashell had his right hand lying idle on his saddle-fork. All he had to do was whip his hand back and he'd have it on his gun.

There was a short silence. Jennie started running toward them from the dug-out, fifty yards north, with Beta running behind her. Jennie cried, "Will please— wait for me, Will!"

Then Fred Bashell said to Mike Arnaiz, "There are ladies present. The order still holds, Mike."

Face bestial and savage, Mike Arnaiz slammed his saw-roweled spurs into his bronc's shoulder, the horse leaping ahead and scattering Arizona dust from steel-shod hoofs. Fred Bashell's pinto swung in behind and the land-locator and his gunman rode hard toward Gila City.

Will said, "The bastards don't even know how to open a wire gate from on horseback," he said. "They had to get off to open an' close it."

Jennie and Beta had arrived. "All you men want to do is fight and then fight some more," Jennie said.

Beta said, "Why didn't you shoot him, Will?"

"Didn't have time," Will said. "You girls scared 'em off. Here's how you open a gate without gettin' off your horse."

He rode close, unlooped the top wire, pulled the gate-post out of the bottom wire, and rode through, opening the gate as he rode. Apache Ike rode through. Then Will reached under his horse's neck, got the gate-post, switched hands, again rode close, poked the bottom in the loop, looped the top—and the gate was closed.

"Looks easy," Jennie said.

"Jus' need practice," Will said. "You got anythin' to eat in the house! Apache an' me's been out all day. Only thing we've had to eat today is breakfast an' a sandwich."

"An' the sandwich was a long ways behind," Apache Ike said.

"We got a jackrabbit stew," Beta said. "Jennie shot first an' missed, an' then it was my shot an' I knocked the jack down."

"When we decide to shoot Bashell an' Arnaiz—or some of their gunmen—I want you on our side, Beta," Will said.

"With pleasure, *Señor* Will. *Con gusto.*"

"We've cooked him for four hours," Jennie said, "but he's still tough, and I thought he was a young one."

Will and Apache Ike went down and walked downhill with the girls. Will looked at Strawberry Springs, a small stream of clear water issuing from gray granite.

Will had never heard of Strawberry Springs going dry. He figured an aquifer carried the water down from some distant range of mountains.

He'd studied water from Uncle Sam's pamphlets. Aquifers were seams in rock that carried water for hundreds of miles underground. He had read where uncle Sam's engineers had colored creek water in the Wyoming mountains and that same colored water had been drawn from Missouri wells years later, having traveled hundreds of miles underground through an aquifer.

All of Hatchet's drinking and cooking water had been hauled by tank from Strawberry, as had all water used for household uses in Gila City. Both the ranch and the town now hauled from Doggone Springs, many miles more in distance.

Gila City's water-tank used to travel to Strawberry Springs, in the morning, fill, and return by early afternoon to Gila City. Now, it took two days to make the round trip to Doggone Springs.

"I'll dish up the jackrabbit stew," Beta said. "You sit right there, Apache Ike, an' talk to me in English, 'cause my English is bad."

"I cain't speak it right myself, *Señorita* Beta," the old man said.

Jennie and Will went to the east fence where Hatchet had three men digging a well, one man being always on rifle-guard. This man came out of the brush as the pair arrived. He carried a Winchester .30-30.

"Any water?" Will asked.

"Yeah, we got water, boss, but it tastes like—" He stopped, red-faced. "Almost said a word I shouldn't, Miss Jennie."

"I probably heard it before," Jennie said. "Think nothing of it, sir."

The digging was shoulder deep. The men worked in water to their waists. The water looked good, although muddy. The men climbed out. One dipped a can of water and handed it to Will, who tasted it gingerly. He immediately spat it out, making a face.

"Worse than vinegar," he said.

One cowboy said, "Worse than the beer you peddle in your saloon, boss."

Will looked at the thirsty cows. They bawled and stood with dogged patience, and Will saw some would soon die. They were on their last legs. He looked at the water coming from the springs and soaking into the ground, a hundred yards east in the Clark homestead.

"We can cut the fence," Jennie said. "I give you my permission."

Will shook his head. "That's not the answer. That would water only a few cows, not Hatchet's eighteen thousand. Hatchet never at any time has had enough water, even with all the springs open. One year we lost around six or eight thousand, to thirst."

"We dug down to granite," a cowpuncher said.

Will frowned thoughtfully. "Where does the water come from?"

"Seeps in through the ground."

"And doesn't come up out of the granite?"

The cowpunchers looked at each other. Both of them shook their heads. "Nope, nothin' comes up outa the granite, boss."

"Why'd you ask?" the other waddy asked.

"Thinkin' of somethin'," Will said. "Seems to be two days to get this water. Either kill Bashell an' Arnaiz, or marry the girl."

Jennie said, *"What?"*

Jennie didn't see his wink.

"Under territorial law, half of what the husban' has is property of the wife," Will said, "an' half of what the wife has is property of the husban', too."

"I'd gladly marry her an' deed you my half, boss," a cowpoke said.

Jennie said, "Never in my life—" She then understood. "Oh, you practical jokers!"

"Jus' an idea," Will said. "An interestin' idea. There's no use goin' any deeper, boys."

"We couldn't if we wanted to, with shovels. It'd take powder to break up this bed of granite."

Will looked at the man. "You ever handle powder, Jackson?" Jackson had punched for Hatchet some three years, memory told Will. During this time he'd kept more or less apart. Will now realized he knew little, or nothing, of the man's life before Jackson had hired out to Hatchet.

"Spent three years as powder-monkey in the Bisbee copper diggin's, boss. There's powder on the ranch. Hid back in a corner, in the storeroom next to the big barn."

Will scowled. "How'd it get there, I wonder? My dad must've used it for somethin', but I can't remember what. I'll ask Apache. He'll know. Anyway, it would be old."

"It's been kept dry, though. I think it'd be good. Mebbeso not as strong as new, but it'd blow the hell out of granite."

Will said, "Tie your shovels onto your saddles an' head for home, men. Gettin' late. Long ride yet."

"What about these cows, boss. They're thirsty."

"I'll haze them over to Doggone. It's still open, I think. Anyway, we'll see."

"Some won't make the trip," Jackson said. "I'll chouse them. Might jus' as well sleep in the saddle as in my bunk. Fact is, I believe the saddle is softer."

"Your chore, then," Will said.

Will and Jennie walked slowly back to the dug-out.

Occasionally, Will tested Strawberry water. The water was alkali all the way to where it came out of the granite and there it was sweet.

"Soil contaminates it inside of ten feet," Will said.

Jennie said, " First, I thought you boys were serious. About being married, you know." She hesitated and blushed slightly. "But the more I think of it, the more I can see it as a means to get water to your cows."

Will looked at her. "Are you serious?"

"Well, I—I could be, Will."

Will put his arm around her shoulders. "Those cows aren't worth that sacrifice, Jennie."

She pushed his arm aside. "I wish I hadn't opened my big mouth," she said. "I just got my foot in it again. Maybe I was thinking about other things than your cattle, Will Cooper?"

Will said, "What a mess a tongue can get humans into, anyway. Here I'm seethin' with things to say—nice things—inside an' not a damned one will come out."

Jennie said, "Let's just walk and say nothing?"

"I feel terrible," Will said. "I feel like I have insulted you. Then, I feel as though you proposed to me an' I turned you down.—"

Jennie cut in with, "I—proposed to you? Hey, isn't that a star coming up over these mountains, way to the east."

"The evening star," Will said. "Venus."

He didn't know whether the star was Mars or Venus or whatever star it was, but he was so nervous he'd said Venus automatically. He was glad when they reached the dug-out, and Beta and Apache Ike.

Apache Ike jokingly said, "Beta jus' proposed marriage to me. I said I was about forty-five years older than she is, but she said it makes no difference—when I get to be a hundred and twenty she'll be seventy-five and what

128

would a mere forty-five years mean then?" He answered his own question. "Absolutely nothin'."

"I never said such a thing," Beta said.

Will almost winced. "I'm ready for a jackrabbit stew," he said.

The moon was up when Hatchet left Strawberry Springs. Jennie had told Will that she'd notified Bashell she would sell her homestead rights.

"He said I couldn't. He knew full well about that fine print we read yesterday. He's foxy, Will."

"What did he say?"

"Said only he could buy my rights, as the contract says. He offered me fifty dollars for them."

"You gonna accept?"

"Definitely not, but I do need money."

"Jose Fernandez needs help in Hatchet's Hardware in Gila City. He told me so the other day. I'll tell him you know all there is to know about hinges, nuts, bolts, and junk like that."

"But I don't know that, Will."

"That makes no difference. You can work there until fall, if you want."

"What happens when fall comes?"

"You can be Gila City's school-teacher, if you want to. Nobody has been signed up for next year's term yet. Hard to get a teacher out here in the wilderness."

"You become our teacher," Beta hurriedly said, "an' I'll start back to school. I quit on the fifth reader."

Now the four of them walked through the warm night to the barbwire gate, Apache Ike and Beta leading, Will and Jennie trailing behind.

Will reached out. He took Jennie's hand. She had a firm small hand, he noticed.

He looked at her. She looked at him. She smiled softly and then looked away. Will Cooper's heart thumped. The world looked a lot better after that smile.

"What a beautiful country," Jennie said.

Yellow moonlight blessed the high desert. For once, there was no wind. Catclaw stood ready with long spines to catch you. Saguaros rose in the silent air.

Distant mountains were gaunt black ridges, hardly discernible but there nonetheless. Smoke trees draped themselves over granite boulders. Night blooming *ocotillo* held scarlet and yellow blossoms.

"I've seen Wyomin' an' Nebraska an' the high grass country," Will said, "but give me the Arizona desert any day of the week and twice on Sunday."

"The air is so clean," Jennie said.

Will said, "Bashell will never take this away from me."

"Amen to that," Apache Ike said.

Chapter Twelve

Fred Bashell had a wagon-load of grub coming down from Tucson. He had sent a rider north to order the clothing, food and other essentials for his farmers.

Each farmer had given him a list of what he wanted. Smith Clark's list had been composed mostly of whiskey and other alcoholic beverages. Bashell had handed the list to this runner and said, "Pay the list no attention. He hasn't got money to pay for that much booze. Buy a nice dress and some other things for the redhead and to hell with the drunken father."

"Like what, boss?"

"Oh, a dress or two. Not too expensive, though."

"Hell, I dunno what size dress she uses."

"Go down to the redlight district. There'll be lots of girls there built about the same size as Jennie. Get the information from one you figure is just Jennie's build."

"I'll do that, gladly. That redhead is a swell looker— An' that form she packs. She could get a shift any time in my whorehouse."

"Never knew you owned a tenderloin joint, Sig."

"I don't, but if I had one, she'd be top girl."

The morning of the day after the double funeral, a young boy rode into town and asked for Fred Bashell. He was a stranger. Bashell's wagon-driver had taken the boy down with him from Tucson. The boy owned a horse. The wagon-driver had sent him ahead to let Bashell know the grub and other things were arriving.

Bashell and Arnaiz rode out to meet the wagon. The two units met at the base of Signal Butte, a high hill rising out of the desert's floor—black-topped and foreboding.

Years ago, during the Indian trouble, Apaches had used the butte as a signal station, flashing in code across the miles of wilderness, mirrors exposed and then shaded—a code that General Nelson A. Miles finally broke. He then learned just where to find the Apaches— and how many composed each war-party.

"See you got a new son," Bashell said.

Sig said, "Picked him up in the redlight district. Mama works there in a crib. Kid wanted to become a cowpuncher an' he had thet ol' nag an' I let him come with me. Maybe he can git a job punchin for Hatchet? I done heard the Coopers has took in a number of young homeless kids to date."

"Cooper won't have Hatchet long," Bashell said.

The boy had ridden back to the wagon ahead of Fred Bashell and Mike Arnaiz. "Done heard Pronto Robbins kissed the dust for good," Sig said. "An' somebody run some lead through thet drunk on Strawberry. Boy heard the news in town an' tol' me."

While Bashell dismounted and opened the tarp to study the things in the wagon, Mike Arnaiz told Sig about Will Cooper gunning down Pronto Robbins and Smith Clark being shot and killed from behind on the hill south of the Cooper ranch-house.

"Never figgered Cooper for a back-shooter," Sig said. "Reckon us homesteaders will have to ride in pairs after this for safety, eh?"

"That'd be a good idea," Arnaiz said.

Bashell finished his inspection. "I guess it's all there," he said. "You bought them dresses for the Clark woman, didn't you?"

Sig had found a prostitute in Tucson that he judged was a duplicate in size to Jennie Clark. "Jennie might have a bit more weight in front, though," he said.

Bashell winked lewdly at Arnaiz. "We'll soon find out who has the biggest pushers," he said. "We'll take over from here, Sig. You can ride double with the boy to your hundred-an'sixty, eh?"

"When'll you be aroun' with my share of the grub?"

Bashel considered. It would take at least two days to distribute the wagon's contents. Sig was homesteading Shotgun Canyon's water-hole. "Be at your location about noon tomorrow," Bashell said.

Sig said slyly, " First the Clark homestead, eh?"

"That's right," Bashell said.

Sig climbed behind the old saddle and he and the boy

133

rode southwest to soon become lost in the wavering heat and wilderness. Bashell and Amaiz tied their broncs behind the wagon and turned the rig east, toward Strawberry Springs.

"Reckon we'll bunk out at Strawberry?" Mike Amaiz said.

"We do, unless the redhead runs us off."

Amaiz seemed interested in the rump of the nigh horse. He was silent for some time and then said, "Ain't none of my business, Fred, but I think it best you don't use force."

"What'd you mean?"

"On the redhead, of course-like you did on that Injun girl, back on the Belle Fourche river."

"She wouldn't come across. I showed her the error of her ways, that's all. Mebbeso somebody should take down the redhead a peg or two, like I did that little Belle Fourche squaw?"

Amaiz wet his lips. He thought of the little Sioux girl, not more than fifteen or so. By now she should have dropped her first colt, Fred Bashell's get. He decided to say no more.

"Got anythin' else to say?" Fred Bashell snarled.

Amaiz shook his head. "Jes' that it's another damn' hot day, boss. Be glad to get some of that cool Strawberry Springs' water."

"Mixed with what?"

"Jus' plain water," Amaiz said.

Beta was alone on the Clark homestead. Jennie had ridden into Gila City, She reported—but she should be back soon, for she had said she'd return before sundown, and sundown was not far off.

"Go to town for supplies?" Fred Bashell asked.

"She never told me why." Beta was fabricating. Jennie had ridden into town to look for work at the Hard-

134

ware Store, as Will Cooper had directed. What Jennie wanted to tell these two was Jennie's business, Beta figured. They'd get nothing out of her.

Beta kept noticing the looks given her by Mike Arnaiz. She knew Fred Bashell was after Jennie. The little Mexican girl didn't like the looks of things. Had it not been for leaving her friend Jennie alone with the two hard-looking men, she'd have silently and quietly and quickly disappeared in the nigh greasewood.

"Here comes somebody from town now," Bashell said.

Beta shaded her eyes. "That's Jennie," she said.

Arnaiz was still worried about Fred Bashell. Bashell didn't seem to realize that he and his cohorts were sitting on a powder keg. Arnaiz couldn't think of a soul in Gila City who were in favor of them. Gila City and its rag-tag populace was completely behind Hatchet.

Arnaiz knew that Bashell had raped the little Belle Fourche Squaw. He hoped Bashell wouldn't try to force either Beta or Jennie. Beta had many relatives in Gila City, some of them tough-looking dark skinned men. Although Jennie hadn't a relative on this range she was still a woman—and the code said that if a woman didn't want a man, that was her right—and the man that forced her could put himself in line for a mob lynching.

Mike Arnaiz realized he was growing tired of being at Fred Bashell's beck and call. This was the third-land-stealing job he'd worked on. He was tired of Bashell, but not tired of the gunman wages Bashell paid him.

Bashell said, "I'll open the gate for her."

He began walking up the hill toward the new fence. Beta said, "He likes Jennie." Her words were merely conversation, nothing else. She trembled inside but refused to show it.

135

"Does she like him?" Mike Arnaiz asked.

"I don't know," Beta hurriedly said. "You'll have to ask her, not me."

Arnaiz looked down at her front. She was very well-developed for her age. "I like you," he said.

Beta wisely did not answer.

Fred Bashell and Jennie walked downhill, the land-locator leading Jennie's mule. He'd noticed immediately that the mule had the Hatchet brand on a shoulder.

"Mr. Cooper left Maude here for me yesterday afternoon," Jennie informed. "He left a mule because he said all the Hatchet horses were more or less green broncs and he was afraid one would throw me off."

"Why didn't you ride one of your work horses?"

"They're both so rough to ride. It's easy to ride Maude. She just hits out and is like a rocking chair."

"I've got a present or two for you," Bashell said.

Jennie bit her bottom lip. She would welcome a present or two, but not from Fred Bashell. She didn't ask what the present was. Bashell noticed this and scowled. Jennie wondered if she and Beta were not in for some trouble, two women located alone out in this Arizona wilderness. She hoped not, especially for Beta's sake.

Beta was no more than a child who had developed physically at too young an age, in Jennie's opinion. Jennie knew how to beat off the would-be fathers, for she'd had much practice with her father's drunken companions back east.

Usually Clark Smith had gone into a drunken sleep, somewhere early in the jags he and his eastern bums staged.

Clark Smith's sudden snoring departure usually seemed to arouse amorous emotions in his fellow alcoholics. Thus, through practice Jennie had learned how to use the toes of her sharp shoes, her thumbs in various parts of a male anatomy, and other forms of rough-and tumble wrestling.

But Beta, she felt sure, didn't know these tactics.

When they arrived at the wagon, Fred Bashell lifted the canvas and came out with two packages, both wrapped in ribbon and gaudy paper. He handed both to Jennie."

Jennie made no more to open them. "Are they both for me?"

"Yes," Bashell said.

Mike Arnaiz stood to one side. Beta stood close to Jennie. Jennie didn't ask what was in the packages. This made Fred Bashell scowl. "Aren't you goin' to open them?" Bashell asked.

Jennie shook her red head. "I never accept gifts from men," she said. She handed back the two packages.

Anger ran across Bashell's jowls. Mike Arnaiz was glad that his boss was not drinking. Had Bashell been boozing he might have grabbed the redhead and forcibly shaken her, he was that angry.

But Fred Bashell caught his anger in time, Arnaiz noticed, and the gunman's muscles relaxed. Bashell spoke to Beta. "Carry the packages into the dug out," he ordered.

Beta looked inquiringly at Jennie. Jennie said, "She's not your servant, Mr. Bashell. She's not mine, either—she's my friend."

Beta said, hesitantly, "They're for Jennie, not me, Mr. Bashell."

Mike Arnaiz almost smiled. His boss was receiving the same kind of treatment from this white girl that he'd received from the Sioux girl. He had a hunch his boss would make the big pitch later and he hoped there'd not be trouble ahead—for he had a feeling he'd side with the two girls.

Bashell put the two packages under the tarp. "Two nice expensive dresses direct from Tuscon," he said. "Well, I'll give them to somebody else, down in town."

"I wish you would." Jennie had small tears in her blue eyes. "I hate to hurt you, Mr. Bashell, but I—Well, I don't want to be indebted to you, or any other man."

"Even Will Cooper?"

"Even Will Cooper," Jennie Clark said.

Bashell said, "We have supplies for you, Miss Jennie. I guess we have a double order, you might say, because the order was placed before your father was murdered by Hatchet."

Jennie almost said, "I'm sure Hatchet never killed my father," but held the words in time. "Again, Mr. Bashell, I hate to hurt you—but I don't want, and don't need, your supplies."

Bashell's narrowed eyes studied her. "What're you goin' t' live on? Desert air and jackrabbits?"

"I'm going to work tomorrow," Jennie said, "and at the end of each day I get paid a dollar, if it's any of your business—and it sure as hell isn't, Fred Bashell."

Bashell stared at her. He'd seen her this angry once before. That had been when she'd held the .22 Marlin at the back of Mike Arnaiz's neck. He was sure, even now, that if Arnaiz had shot against Will Cooper, Jennie would have shot Arnaiz dead in his boots.

Fred Bashell said soothingly, "Let's all hold our horses, eh? This is nothin' to get in a scrap about, Miss Jennie. Do they have a school session in the summer in Gila City?"

"I'm going to work with *Señor* Fernandez in the Hardware."

Fred Bashell knew that Cooper—and Hatchet—

138

owned the Gila City Hardware, just as Hatchet owned every business in town. He knew Jose Fernandez only worked in the store for Hatchet.

Will Cooper had evidently given this redhead the job. Bashell doubted if the Hardware did enough business to merit hiring another hand and common sense told him this woman knew little—if anything—about the hardware business.

Will Cooper was sure beating the pants off him regarding this delectable little redheaded hunk of femininity. Fred Bashell then realized he'd more or less taken this redhead for granted, thinking sooner or later she'd come around of her own accord.

The death of her father had changed this situation. When Smith Clark had been alive, this redhead had been more or less under her father's domination, but now that her father was gone she was her own boss and stubborn.

He had wished quite a few times that he'd not trailed Smith Clark to the Cooper ranch and pumped those three .45 bullets into the drunk's back. He'd deliberately waylaid Clark that night when Clark had left the saloon, flat broke and dead drunk.

Clark had said he was heading on foot for Hatchet. "Gonna make peace with Cooper," he'd said. "Nice young man. An' mebbeso I kin bum some money off him, who knows?" And he'd winked lewdly—and drunkenly—there in the lamplight streaming from one of the saloon's rear windows.

And Smith Clark had staggered northwest through the chamise toward Hatchet. And Mike Arnaiz, who'd been hidden in the high greasewood, had said, "Your job or mine, boss?"

"I'll take care of the drunken bastard."

"Then me to my bunk," Mike Arnaiz had said.

Bashell had expected the ambush murder of Smith Clark to throw the blame of the drygulching onto Hatchet. How was he to know the Hatchet guard didn't pack a .45, but packed a Winchester?

Men on this range were supposed to tote .45s, not carry rifles. The whole thing had gone sour. Gila City residents were sure Hatchet had not shot the farmer from behind.

Sheriff Emil Dickinson, if he turned his attention to Mussampa, would also side with Hatchet, he felt sure. He'd met Dickinson a few times in Tucson. Dickinson had not been too friendly. His attention was directed back to Jennie when she said to Beta, "I'm hungry."

"*Libreotra vez,*" Beta said. "Jackrabbit again."

Fred Bashell said, "Plenty of grub in the wagon. Didn't know I was a cook, did you, Miss Jennie?"

"I sure didn't."

Bashell went to work over a small fire built outside by Arnaiz and Beta. Jennie changed clothes inside the dugout. Bashell hadn't given up. He'd heard that the way to a man's heart was through his stomach. Maybe the old axiom could be reversed to read, the way to a woman's heart was through her stomach?

His Bowie knife sliced off thick slices of Iowa ham he'd ordered for his own table. He fried spuds a delicate brown. Coffee sent out its aroma into the clean desert air.

All ate with gusto.

"This desert air sure gives one an appetite," Jennie said.

Bashell speared ham with his knife. "I think of things too late, Miss Jennie. I should have got you when you came to be my stenographer. Is it too late?

Jennie said, "I promised *Señor* Fernandez, Mister Bashell, and I can't go back on my word."

"Think it over," the land-locator said. "I'll put the wages at a buck twenty-five a day."

Jennie knew that a quarter a day meant quite a raise in wages. She also knew that Bashell needed a secretary no more than she needed a wild Hatchet bronc.

She'd suspected that Will Cooper had offered her the job at the hardware only to help her out. She'd questioned *Señor* Fernandez rather closely on this point.

She'd become assured the *Señor* needed a bookkeeper. He'd shown her his records, piled in a dusty corner, and she'd then realized she had at least two months work just straightening out old records.

Señor Fernandez needed her, she knew for sure. Had he not, she'd not have taken the job.

"You should have spoken before, Mister Bashell," she said. "It's too late now. I never go back on a promise."

"Sorry," Bashell said.

Beta and Jennie washed the tinware after the meal and then all four walked east to where Hatchet had dug for water—and gotten only alkali and gypsum. Hatchet cows stood bawling, flanks gaunt. Two cows were down, apparently for the last time—and three lay dead, bloated and covered by flies. Overhead buzzards circled, waiting for the nosy humans to leave—for they'd been tearing the entrails from a freshly-dead calf.

Bashell climbed through the barbwire and scooped up a handful of water and tasted it. He immediately grimaced and spit it out. "No animal could drink that," he said, gloatingly.

Jennie looked at the suffering animals. In her opinion, innocent animals—or children—should not suffer because of adults. Then she remembered that Will had told her not to cut the fence. She sent a brief look at tough Fred Bashell; then at stoic, gunhung Mike Arnaiz.

And she again remembered this was not the tame, easy-going midwest. This was the tough frontier between the territory of Arizona and the Yaqui state of Sonora, old Mexico.

Fred Bashell gambled for a small fortune. He'd not let anybody stand in his way. She felt sure either Bashell—or Arnaiz—had murdered her father to get him out of the way for even though he'd not been much, her father had stood between her and Bashell, if Bashell wanted to use violence.

She realized she and Beta were in a precarious position. Beta's worried glances told her the Mexican girl was also fully aware of the circumstances.

Bashell climbed back through the barbwire, Arnaiz separating the strands so his boss wouldn't get hung upon the sharp barbs. Bashell looked at the thirsty cows.

"Let 'em die," he said.

Beta looked at Jennie. Jennie looked at Beta. Beta opened her mouth, plainly to protest; but Jennie, unnoticed by either Bashell or Arnaiz, shook her head slightly. Beta closed her mouth.

The wagon still contained the bedrolls Sig and the boy had used on the trip down. The four sat and talked for a while in front of the dug-out. Darkness came tiptoeing across the desert, wrapping it in mystic soft folds of night. Finally Jennie said, "I got to get to bed. I have to be in town on the job by seven in the morning."

She and Beta stood hidden in the dark doorway and watched Bashell and Arnaiz take bedrolls from the wagon. They carried these to the spring and went into the brush.

Beta whispered, "What do you suppose he was going

to give you, *patrona?*"

"I don't know," Jennie said, "and I don't care. But I do know you and I have to get out of here—and leave as soon as possible."

"I would have sneaked off when they first came," Beta said, "but I couldn't leave you behind."

Jennie groped and found Beta's hand. "I like you, too, Beta."

The Mexican girl sobbed quielty. "I like you too, *Señorita* Jennie. But in an hour, comes the moon, no?"

"Where shall we go?" Jennie asked.

"Out on the desert. We take only one blanket, each. The desert is not savage, like some people think. The desert is kind, if you know the desert. Many times we all go out on the desert—my family and others—and we have a fire, and we roast *chivo*—Goat—and we sleep out on the sand."

"Have patience," Jennie said.

Both Mike Arnaiz and Fred Bashel came silently into the dug-out around midnight, the moon brilliant and the desert dappled with color and shadows—and with the sad lowing of thirsty Hatchet cattle.

Bashell led the way, Arnaiz a pace behind. The dug-out was inky black. Neither man heard anybody breathing. Bashell knew the dug-out's interior well. He felt and found a cast-iron bed, the one he knew Jennie slept in.

The bed was empty.

His fingers withdrew. He went to the other bed, the one Smith Clark had slept on. Again, fingers groped; again, they found no human.

" For god's sake, Mike, light the lamp."

"Where is it?"

"Light a sulphur. Look for the damn' thing."

The match flared. It showed the lamp sitting on the

small table. It also showed each bed to be empty.

Arnaiz lit the lamp. He restored the clean chimney. The lamp lighted the cave completely.

"They're gone," Arnaiz said.

"Any damn' fool can see that!" Fred Bashell snarled. "I must have dozed off a few minutes, when I watched this thing from the bresh!"

"Moonlight's awful bright," Mike Arnaiz said. "Shall we try to trail 'em, boss?"

Bashell looked about. He couldn't see Jennie's Marlin .22 rifle. And usually it rested in yon corner, butt down.

"T'hell with 'em," Bashell said.

Chapter Thirteen

Water-holes were miles apart on this Mussampa range. It took two days for Bashell to deliver all the supplies. The first homestead was on Wineglass Springs. Jim Warden held down there.

Bashell's mind was made up. "We leave these homesteads an' gather Hatchet cattle, Jim. You're wagon boss. I'll tell all the boys along the route. They'll meet here at your shack. There's five hundred bucks to the gun that kills Will Cooper. Two hundred for the one that knocks down the ol' Injun."

"Good news, boss. I'm tired of settin' here on my behin' doin' nothin'. But what'll we do with the cows we gather?"

"I'll tell you later. Day after tomorrow I'll meet you an' the herd—at Gassman Springs."

"We'll be there."

The wagon moved on. Arnaiz said, "If they're leavin', why then are we deliverin' these supplies?"

"Jus' made up my mind. This has drug on too long. Let the coyotes eat the grub. Or the packrats stow it away."

Hank Snowden was on Kitchen Springs. "Glad you made up your mind, Fred. Anythin's better'n goin' loco on this damn' sand."

"I'm saddlin' up an' pullin' north to Warden's shack right now," Bill Mullins said. He'd homesteaded Yaqui Wells.

They drove south to Ed Kilnor who held down Mad Sagehen Springs. "Why don't we jus' forget the damn' cows an' storm the Hatchet home-ranch an' burn it to the ground?"

Bashell shook his head. "If this herd deal I got in mind backlashes, we can blame it on Will Cooper— tellin' everybody he tried to run the cows over us, not us over him."

Kilmor shrugged. "Don't understan' it all, but what you say is okay with me, Fred. No need to leave much here. From what you say, I figger me an' this mud shack has parted company forever, thank God."

"We're leavin' jus' a mite of grub at each homestead," Arnaiz said.

Fred Bashell said, "We'll donate what's left over to the scissorbills in Gila City. Help make them on our side, mebbe."

Max Martin homesteaded Black Rock Springs. The

spring was almost dry. Only a small trickle of sweet water oozed out of the granite seam.

Hatchet cows bawled outside the six-wire barbwire fence. Bashell smiled as he saw the bloated carcasses of about a hundred dead Hatchet cows.

Buzzards were having a wonderful time. Arnaiz remarked that buzzards must have some way of alerting other buzzards when a feast presented itself. "Must be buzzards there all the way from California," he said.

"An' mebbeso New Mexico an' west Texas," Max Martin said.

"Good perfume," Arnaiz said, wrinkling his nose. "Wind blows right acrost them t'ord this shack, too. How do you stan' it, Max?"

Max Martin was saddling his bronc to head for Jim Warden's shack and the coming beef gather. "I don't stick aroun' the shack. I hide out back in the bresh, where the stink cain't reach me. Only reason I'm at the shack now was I saw you boys comin'."

Martin swung into leather.

"See you day after tomorrow at Gassman," Fred Bashell told the gunman.

"I'll be there." Max Martin gave his bronc the rowels. The horse's shod hoofs threw back gravel and sand. Within a few minutes, the gunman was out of sight in the high *chaparral*.

"Seems happy to pull out," Arnaiz said.

Fred Bashell looked about. Sparse desert grass grew along the bases of desert plants where what little moisture there was stayed longer, because of the shade.

He looked at the bony, dying cows. He smelled the stench of the rotting carcasses. He looked up at the blue sky without a cloud. Sweat trickled down his jowls.

"Do you blame him?" he asked.

Mike Arnaiz smiled.

Fred Bashell felt as though a weight had left him. He'd made up his mind out of the blue, and now that action and an end lay ahead he felt relieved. He wished now he'd have hit Hatchet right after settling his gunmen on Hatchet water. Or even before that, when he and his gunmen had ridden into Gila City. But hindsight, he knew, was always better than foresight.

"Mind tellin' me jus' what you got in mind, boss?" Mike Arnaiz asked.

"Not a bit. Hatchet is diggin' outside the Strawberry Springs fence, as you know. We get a big herd—say two or three thousand Hatchet cows—an' we jus' stampede them over the Hatchet crew."

"What if Cooper isn't with the crew?"

"We'll make sure he is, before we start firin' an' hollerin' behin' the herd. Them cattle are gaunt and poor, but ringy as hell. They're mad, Mike, an' they're ready to run—an' run over anythin' in their way."

"I know that," Arnaiz said. "But still, what if Cooper ain't with the crew? What then?"

"We ride against Hatchet's home-ranch."

"I want thet five hundred," Mike Arnaiz said.

Fred Bashell sent a glance at Arnaiz. Arnaiz sounded rather false. Bashell had never really trusted the stoic gunman. He realized that was only logical.

In this game, you trusted nobody—but yourself. And then, at times, you even doubted your own person.

"An if I don't knock off Cooper," Arnaiz said, "I'll settle for the ol' Injun an' two hundred."

"We'd better move on," Bashell said. "Only one more to warn an' that's Sig Nelson."

The wagon ground on. Mike Arnaiz rolled a Bull Durham wheat-straw cigaret. He looked up at tall Signal Butte to the northeast. "Man could be up there watchin' us now with field glasses, boss."

148

Bashell glanced at the Butte, at least thirty miles away. " Field glasses couldn't pick us out this far away, even in this clear air."

"But a telescope could," Mike Arnaiz said.

Bashell laughed. "Who's got a telescope on this range?"

He didn't know that Hatchet had a powerful telescope. Abe Cooper had bought it years before, when he'd trailed cattle into Los Angeles for sale, the year before the railroad built through Tucson.

Abe Cooper had bought the telescope to install it in his high *mirador*, a tower he and almost every border *rancho* possessed.

From this high tower a man could see for miles around. There'd been Apache and Yaqui trouble on this desert when Abe had moved in Hatchet cattle, and the telescope brought the range of a man's vision much closer.

The *mirador* was four stories high, but still it lacked the height to allow a man to see more than ten miles or so from the *hacienda*. This had been range enough for the Indian trouble, but not to see the entire sweep of Hatchet's huge range.

Right now that telescope, mounted on a home-made stand, was watching from Signal Butte.

The stand had been made by Apache Ike at the ranch's forge. The old Indian had carried the telescope to the top of the Butte. Right now, Apache Ike's eye was glued to the telescope's small end. Years ago his ancestors had squatted here—sans telescope or field-glasses—and watched enemy war-parties moving below. He was reverting back to his past, with a man-made assistant.

He was a Chiricahua Apache of the tribe of Geronimo. He'd seen that the redman could never hope to whip the white, and as a youth he'd quit his tribe and wandered into the Texas Panhandle. He'd learned early that after abandoning his tribe, he belonged neither to the redman or the white.

Finally he wandered into Hatchet, there on the *Llanos Estacados*. Abe Cooper apparently didn't care if a man was white or black or red, just so he did his work and earned his pay honestly.

Since then, he'd never left Hatchet. When Abe had died he'd switched his allegiance to Abe's son. He had little—if anything—to do with Anna Cooper. He had long considered her beyond hope. He often wondered how a man as sensible as Abe could have married such an eccentric female.

He'd wondered many times where and how Abe had met the woman destined to be his wife. But his old friend had never offered to give him details and he'd be the last one on earth to ask.

As years passed, he become more and more silent and to himself. The only one he really spoke to was Will, and he'd never had a son or any get. More and more, Will became precious to him.

He was afraid that Will would get killed in this battle for water. He knew that Fred Bashell, Mike Arnaiz and the Bashell gunmen would fight to the bitter end. He had a feeling that a large sum of money awaited Bashell and his gundogs, if proud Hatchet were finally brought to its knees.

He knew he would do everything in his power to make sure Will Cooper kept on living. He knew that soon his life would end, for the years were heavy on his stooped shoulders. Far better he be killed than Will.

He had little, if any, use for women. He'd never married and never had the slightest inclination to do so. He was sure that some men were born to live single lives. Their natures demanded such. He was also sure he'd been born one such man.

He was handy with tools. Upon his shoulders fell all the *ranch's* repair jobs. He was the spread's combined blacksmith and saddle-maker. He more or less lived in the big barn's haymow. Here, he had his work-bench and tools. He liked to be alone.

Thus, his self-appointed job of watching from the high top of Signal Butte pleased him. It served two purposes. First, it aided Will Cooper and Hatchet and, secondly, it gave him privacy.

He went onto the butte's top the evening of the day he'd shot down Frank Hoffard. He now wished he'd killed the Bashell gunman. He'd heard, before leaving town after the funeral, that Fred Bashell had upped the ante on Will Cooper's life to five hundred dollars.

That was a big sum on a range where a cowpuncher was lucky to get a job with two private saddle-horses and his bedding, paying twenty bucks a month and found.

Most cowpunchers had never had that much money in their lives, he knew—and he also knew most never had any hopes of making such a big sum. Which told him that ahead of Bashell—if he got control of Mussampa—lay a large sum of money, for a man as tight-fisted as Bashell didn't throw his money around without being sure of a good return.

He told Will where he was going, and what he was going to do, and he left the ranch with his rifle and shot-gun and plenty of ammunition. His rifle was a Model 1873 Winchester bored for .44/40 cartridges, the same caliber of his Colt revolver. Thus, he carried only the one caliber of ammunition.

And he also carried the telescope and its tripod. The telescope was the collapsible type; thus, it was easy to

151

transport.

He walked up the dim trail leading to the butte's crown, thinking of the many mocassins over the centuries that had also trod this same path, now almost grown over with brush. No longer did the Apache roam and fight and kill for the land the whites had stolen from him, through the use of better instruments of death and the sheer overpowering of superior numbers.

He had nothing against the whites. He had nothing for them, either. He realized the Indian—his race—was and had been a stupid bunch. They'd not even had sense enough to invent a wheel, even after they'd seen round rocks roll hell-bent down steep hillsides.

The white man was smarter than the redman. That had been—and was—the whole answer, in his way of thinking. The white man didn't accept things. When something disagreed with him—and his way of living—he corrected that point as soon as possible, to the best of his ability.

He asked questions. The Indian didn't. The white-man sought ways to make things better, even to ways of killing his enemies. The Indian just accepted things and let it go at that.

And because of his failings, the redskin had been easily conquered by the whites. But this was in the scheme of things. He'd long ago reasoned that all things, no matter how strong, had to eventually fall, and die.

Hatchet would someday follow this rule. Due to the passages of time and the events time brought about, Hatchet too would fall. But there was one fly in the soup, according to his thinking—the right time had not come for Hatchet to march on into history.

That time, in his estimation, would come later.

Because he had lived long with the whites—and

because he was Indian in blood—his outdoor lore consisted of knowledge learned by watching and doing, and by instinct.

Cottonwood rabbits abounded on top of the butte. Here, shallow recesses that wind and time had cut in the huge sandstone rocks held water for many months. He also knew tht cottontails got water from the roots of plants they ate. And those recesses back in the rocks in the shade undoubtedly held a bit of water all the year around.

He always carried a few yards of fine silk thread in a saddle-bag. He used it for sutures on horses and cattle deeply cut by falling against rocks, and now cut by barbwire.

This thread made good rabbit-snares. You set a loop in a rabbit runway and invariably, within a short time, it snared a cottontail. The rabbit, in fighting the loop, usually strangled himself to death.

He packed two canteens of fresh water. He knew just how much water a horse needed each day. He also knew this water was hidden in pools on top of the granite boulders, back in the rocks. There, the sun could not get at it. Thus, there was little evaporation there.

He had shielded the front lens of the telescope. It had been easy to do. With his tinsnips he'd cut an Arbunkle coffee can in two parts; the one part fitted over the end of the telescope, held solidly by a thick buckskin strap. Thus, the lens could not cast reflection.

He saw Sig Nelson, the boy and the wagons meet Fred Bashell and Mike Arnaiz at the base of Signal Butte. He saw Bashell and his gunman take over the wagons and make their first stop at Strawberry Springs. He saw only Beta on the springs.

He saw Sig Nelson and the boy ride double to Nelson's homestead shack, a mud hut miles away to the west. He saw Jennie Clark leave Gila City and ride to her homestead. Fred Bashell walked out to open the gate for her and to greet her.

Bashell, Arnaiz, Beta and Jennie were now two women and two men on Strawberry Springs. And old Apache Ike scowled.

Should he ride down and tell Will?

He abandoned this plan. Jennie was old enough to take care of herself and Jennie undoubtedly would watch out for Beta. Night came and below him in the endless space glowed tiny yellow lights—the kerosene lamps of the gunmen posing as homesteaders.

Southeast lay the lights of Gila City. One by one the lamps and lanterns were extinguished, and soon the moonlight claimed the wilderness. The night was torrid, the breeze blisteringly hot.

The wind howled in the sandstones. He dozed off and when he opened his eyes dawn was walking with silent boots across the rangelands below, the *chamiso* and *saguaro* throwing shadows to the west.

He saw Bashell and Arnaiz harnessing their team to the supply wagon, but he saw no sign of Beta or Jennie, and he scowled. He scanned the area between Strawberry Springs and Gila City, and he caught the two women walking toward the town, keeping always in the highest brush.

He grinned.

He saw Hatcht ride to Strawberry Springs. Will Cooper rode in the lead of a wagon and team with five Hatchet cowboys. Bashell and Arnaiz had already left Strawberry; they and their rig and animals moving northwest toward the first gunman-farmer's settlement.

Hatchet was digging further on the well outside of Jennie's fence. Apache Ike held his glasses for a long moment on the thirsty cows standing below Jennie's barbwire.

Some were trying to drink the soda and gypsum water bubbling from the top of the well into the ditch. They did not drink much, Apache Ike noticed. They lowered their muzzles but for a few minutes, if that long.

He put his telescope on Hatchet two miles to the southwest. A few men moved in the yard, but the *rancho* showed little, if any activity. Will had ordered his riders not to ride range and they were obeying his orders.

Sadly, slowly, the wiry old buck shook his head. Will was caught between the devil and the pitchfork. The boy didn't know just which way to jump. But when he did jump, Apache Ike knew it would be a gunsmoky leap. It had to be. There could be no other.

Thereupon, when he used his telescope, he kept track of the supply wagon as it moved from farmer to farmer, like a small dark dot weaving its way through *chamise* and catclaw and ghost-trees.

Hatchet worked on the well. He saw the crew *siesta* for two hours during the most torrid afternoon heat. When dusk came he saw Jennie and Beta walk out of Gila City, heading for Strawberry Springs.

A tall man and a youth walked with them. Both of the males carried rifles. Apache Ike caught the reflection of the sun on the firearms. He judged them to be old and worn weapons.

For almost all arms here were blue-steeled when new. Only the old weapons had the blue worn off.

He recognized the men as Beta's father and oldest brother, Carlos. And he grinned. The girls had sneaked out on Bashell and Arnaiz, had slept in the brush, and now had guards.

He saw Jennie stop at the well-digging crew. She talked with Will, and Apache Ike wondered if Hatchet was not being asked to cut the Clark fence. Apache Ike looked northeast.

A small dust cloud hung about ten miles northeast. His telescope showed that some of the would-be farmers were hazing Hatchet cattle. They were working up a small herd of Hatchet stock.

Why?

Apparently, they were pointing the cattle toward Strawberry. Suddenly the old man's frown disappeared, and he understood.

The farmers were forcing the issue. They undoubtedly would drive Hatchet stock forcibly through the Clark fence. Bashell would then have reason to move against Hatchet, either by calling in the sheriff or by smoking short-guns and booming rifles.

Then, the frown returned.

No Hatchet men rode range? He had seen none leave the ranch. Will was making an error there—a serious error.

For Will should have had his scouts out, watching the farmers. He judged at least two days more for the gather to be big enough to stampede through Strawberry Springs barbwire...if Strawberry Springs was the selected spot to hit.

He knew he was guessing at a number of points that time might prove to be false. He'd best wait and tomorrow would tell more. Time would reveal the meaning of the scenes being enacted below.

Late that afternoon, the supply wagon reached Sig Nelson's farm. Apache Ike saw Sig and the boy come out to meet Bashell and Arnaiz. After delivering supplies to Nelson, the wagon turned straight east toward Gila City.

The last of the farmers had received his rations.

A short while later, a small figure led a horse into the brush behind the Nelson wickiup. The figure mounted and rode fast through the chaparral, heading northeast toward Hatchet's home-ranch.

Apache Ike finally recognized, the horse and rider. The rider was the boy who had come out with the supply wagon. He rode the old skate he and Nelson mounted, after turning over the wagon to Bashell and Amaiz.

The boy rode into the Hatchet yard, the guard stopping him and going in with him, another cowpuncher coming out to replace the original guard. And again the old Indian scowled.

He remembered other homeless waifs riding into Hatchet and out of the goodness of Abe Cooper's heart, they'd been given work, a roof, grub and clothes. Was this boy seeking similar treatment? Or had he been sent over to spy on Hatchet?

The boy unsaddled his cob. He went with the guard into the cookshack. Apache Ike knew he was getting fed. Hatchet apparently had another orphan? Or another spy?

Time would tell which.

Apparently, Hatchet had spent the day driving down a length of old well-casing—twelve-inch stuff— that Abe had used years ago, when he'd tried to dig for water. Apache Ike remembered a case of dynamite. It was in a corner in the old storeroom, behind the barn.

Hank Jackson had been a powder-monkey in the Bisbee copper diggings to the east, he remembered Jackson saying. Evidently Hatchet was pushing the solid steel case through granite by force.

The casing would then be loaded with dynamite. What happened when the black powder exploded was in the hands of *Dios,* or somebody or something.

Apache Ike dined on broiled cottontail. He knew how to make a fire that emitted very little, if any, smoke. He squatted and dozed, and again the sunrise awakened him.

His telescope showed that Fred Bashell and Mike Arnaiz had made camp in the high chaparral, about fifteen miles west of town. They were now busy harnessing their horses which had been picketed out in the brush.

Bashell men were moving Hatchet cattle. They had them pointed toward Strawberry Springs, for sure. The telescope showed the young boy feeding the chickens. Anna Cooper worked on her roses behind the ranch-house.

She wore a huge black sunbonnet and a flowing black dress. Apache Ike idly wondered why she wore black. Black attracted the heat and the sun was becoming very, very hot again.

She surely still couldn't be in mourning over Abe. Apache Ike grinned. He remembered her not even attending Abe's funeral in Gila City. She had, in fact, seemed rather relieved when Abe had gone over the ridge.

She's just lately started wearing all black.

Again the work-wagon left Hatchet, heading southwest for Strawberry Springs. Will Cooper rode quite a distance ahead. He led a pack horse. Apache Ike understood.

The pack-horse carried the dynamite. If it exploded and blew everything to smithereens the rest of the crew, at that safe distance, would not go up in a roar, but Will and the two horses would.

Apache Ike shook his head. Will Cooper was of the same mold as had been Abe Cooper.

Not by accident did he lead the animal carrying the black powder. He'd not put a Hatchet hand in such danger. Rather than endanger the life of a hireling, he'd take the risk himself.

Apache Ike looked beyond the Hatchet work-crew to Strawberry Springs. Jennie and Beta were riding to town double on old Maud, Beta behind and holding a rifle. Beta's father and brother stayed at the homestead. They walked down and met the Hatchet men. Soon, they were working with the Hatchet crew.

Bashell and Arnaiz hit the wagon-road some four miles ahead of the girls, and old Maude. Apache Ike saw a rider leave town, heading west toward the homesteads. The telescope showed a patch of white on one of the rider's shoulder. That arm was in a sling.

He recognized Frank Hoffard. Evidently Doc Martinez had given Hoffard permission to ride home. Hoffard met the Bashell wagon a mile west of town. There were no preliminaries.

Bashell and Arnaiz used rifles. When they drove on, Hoffard lay still and apparently dead to the side of the trail. Bashell and Arnaiz drove off, but not until after Bashell had searched Hoffard's pockets and saddlebags.

Whatever he found, he put into his pockets before climbing onto the wagon's high-spring seat.

Apache Ike remembered the gold in Pronto Robbins' possession. Will Cooper had beaten Bashell to that blood-money. But evidently Bashell had recovered the sum he'd paid Frank Hoffard.

Now, locals would lay the blame of Hoffard's killing on Hatchet.

Apache Ike watched Jennie and Beta ride old Maude down on the dead man. Jennie halted old Maude for a moment. Neither girl went down. Then Jennie rode hurriedly toward Gila City, Beta beating Maude with a small switch.

Apache Ike looked back at the gathering herd.

If the herd was heading for Strawberry Springs it should reach there about tomorrow evening, he figured—and would run to some three thousand odd head of Hatchet longhorns.

Bashell and Arnaiz drove into Gila City. He saw the wagon stop at Bashell's office outside of town. Within a few minutes, Jennie and Beta and old Maude arrived.

Rigs and people on foot immediately started out west, heading for Hoffard's carcass. Or had the man merely been wounded?

Apache Ike grinned. Hoffard was dead. Had he not been dead, Bashell would not have left him—he'd have sent other bullets into the gunman.

And if Hoffard had merely been wounded, Jennie and Beta would have dismounted to help him, Apache Ike felt sure.

Soon the body was in a buggy, heading back toward town, Hoffard's saddle-horse being led to town by a man on horseback. The cavalcade entered town. Soon, a man rode out of town fast for Hatchet.

He was going to tell Will of Hoffard's death, Apache Ike figured. The man didn't spend much time on the ranch. He was soon heading southwest through the *malpais* toward Strawberry Springs.

The hot afternoon slowly passed. Apache Ike was glad to see that nobody from Hatchet left Strawberry Springs to ride into town. Gila City would be in a state of anxiety, he guessed. Some might even think that Will—or some Hatchet man—had indeed ambushed Frank Hoffard.

Bashell would be busy expounding the theory that Hatchet had murdered one-armed Frank Hoffard. Bashell might even be claiming that the damn' ol' Indian might have waylaid Hoffard, to finish what he'd started the other day and hadn't successfully ended.

Apache Ike left Signal Butte's top at dusk. He'd seen the boy ride over to Strawberry Springs on old Flip, an ancient gray saddle-horse that Will Cooper kept because his father had once had Flip as his top horse.

Evidently the boy was on an errand for Anna Cooper, for Apache Ike had seen her covertly leave the back door of the ranch-house and accost the boy in the brush, where the ranch-hands couldn't see her.

Before leaving, he gave the herd another scrutiny. The gunmen had the cattle in Gassman Coulee. There was water there—under a fence—and the cattle could be bedded there, after the farmer settling there had left them water.

He walked down the trail, leading his horse, carefully picking his path in the dusk, for if an old man's boots slipped on the pebbles and he fell and broke a bone—

An old man's bones healed slowly, if at all...

Chapter Fourteen

The new boy returned from Strawberry Springs ahead of the Hatchet well-drilling crew. Apache Ike met him a mile southwest of the ranch's headquarters.

The boy dragged Flip to a halt. "An Injun!" He wheeled the old nag and hammered his ribs with his heels. Apache Ike rode in and caught the reins just above the snaffle bit, to stop the proceedings.

The boy said, "I'm jus' a boy, Injun. I'm—I don't wanna be scalped!" He trembled with fear, face ashen.

Apache Ike smiled. "I'm Apache Ike," he explained.

"I'm *segundo*—second in command—on Hatchet."

"Apache—Ike?"

"That's right. I won't hurt you, boy. You'll save me a trip to Strawberry Springs. How is the well-diggin' comin' along?"

"I heard them talk about you at the springs. Somebody said maybe you'd killed a man named Hoffard, or sumpthin' like that."

"Who said that?"

"Couple of the Hatchet cowboys. But they laughed when they said it. I think they was jus' jokin'. You sure scared me, Mister Ike. I'm from back east, in Pennsylvania."

"How come you work for Hatchet?"

"How'd you know I'm a Cooper hand?"

Apache Ike realized he'd slipped his tongue. He remedied it by saying, "You never saw me at the ranch, but I saw you this mornin', when I rode out to look at some cattle."

The boy told about freighting in with Sig Nelson. He hadn't liked Nelson and he'd run across a Mexican wood-cutter in the brush, who'd told him where Hatchet was located and that hatchet had a way of picking up stray boys and turning them into first-class cowpunchers and bronc-stompes. "An' I wanna be both of them, Mister Ike."

"What reason did you have to ride to the Springs?"

"The lady in black—she sent me. Thet's Missus Cooper, ain't she? Mamma of Will, the boss?"

Apache Ike nodded. "What did she want to know from the Springs?"

"She wanted to know how the diggin' was gettin' along, an' things like that. I don't know why she sent me. She could talk to her son, couldn't she?"

"I guess so. How is the diggin'?"

"They got the pipe deep into the granite, I heard them say. Hard job, pick an' hammers, but they got it anchored. Now they put dynamite in it an' let 'er go."

"When will thet happen, son?"

"About tomorrow sunset, Mister Cooper said. Say, what's gonna happen here, anyway? Everybody packs a gun on his hip-some have two—an' they never git far from their horses or their rifles."

"You got good eyes, boy."

"It's like them wild-west stories I used to read back east. I'd make out like I was studying a big book, but inside I'd have a western story book—all about guns an' cowboys. Jus' like here."

"I'll ride to the ranch with you," Apache Ike said.

Will and the work-crew and wagon came in around nine. Will and Apache Ike confabbed in Apache Ike's haymow. Both big hay-doors were open at each end of the mow and because of the height, a welcome breeze—although very small—cooled things a trifle.

The old Indian reported all events he'd seen from his high aerie. Will Cooper listened with a quiet, studious face. Will looked up when the Apache reported that Bashell had murdered Frank Hoffard.

Will said, " For two things, he killed a fellow human—to lay the blame on Hatchet an' get his money back. You know, I got a hunch Bashell shot Clark from behin', too."

"Got any proof?"

"*Señora* Gonzalez an' Manuel Rios got drunk yesterday. No, not on *vino*, but on peyote. Manuel told her that the night Smith Clark got killed, he'd been in the brush behin' the saloon."

"Doin' what?"

Will smiled. "Prob'ly lookin' for some peyote roots. The town council has a law against peyote use, you

164

know—so he might have sneaked out an' got down on his han's an' knees an' felt aroun'.''

Manuel Rios was the town wood-cutter. He grubbed out the bulbous roots of *chamisal* and greasewood and sold them, by so much a kilogram, to his neighbors. Somehow he kept himself and his fat wife and fourteen children in *tortillas* and *frijoles.*

"What else, boss?"

"Well, he tol' Missus Gonzalez that he saw a man stagger out of the saloon, and the man said, 'I'm headin' out for Hatchet. Mebbeso I kin borrow some money from Will Cooper to buy another drink. No damn' credit in this damn' saloon,' or somethin' like that.' ''

"An' *Señora* Gonzalez tol' you, Will?''

"No, she tol' Jennie in the Hardware store today. Jennie said the ol' girl's eyes were big as saucers."

"Peyote," Apache Ike said. "Go on."

The rest of the story was simple. Manuel Rios had frozen in his tracks, listening; for brush had crackled at his right, as Smith Clark had been swallowed by the night.

"Manuel tol' Gonzalez he'd heard a man say he was gonna follow Clark. The man spoke English, which is uncommon in town—everybody there jus' speaks Tex-Mex."

"He didn't know who the man was? He never saw him?"

"Night was too dark, he tol' Gonzalez. Nope, he didn't know who spoke, but he said he heard two different men-both speakin' English."

Apache Ike considered this. "Did Jennie talk to Manuel?"

"She went to this shack during *siesta* period today. She said he was full of somethin', an' she guessed it was peyote. His wife and kids were without grub. She couldn't get a word out of him about anythin', she told me."

"That fits in," Apache Ike said.

"So Jennie went to the merc. She tol' them there how the Rios kids and missus hadn't a *friple* or *brtilla* in the house. So some grub went over to 'em, right away. Manuel's a good hand when he don't hit the root."

"That proves nothin'," Apache Ike said. "The new boy—He tol' me your mother'd sent him out to Strawberry to see how the work was gettin' along."

Will shook his head. "I never did understand Anna Cooper, but since she went to that funeral—an' none of them stiffs was kin or worked for Hatchet—I didn't know."

"It could be that the new boy is a spy for Bashell," Apache Ike said. "He come in with thet Nelson would-be farmer, you know."

"He's bein' watched. I've alerted Slim an' Smoky an' Jake to keep an eye on him."

"What about the herd they're gatherin', boss?"

Will considered that angle thoughtfully. "From what you say, it could only be driven with Strawberry as the end—'cause Strawberry's the only spring ahead. I'd say Bashell is pushin' things. Could you tell me why?"

"I think Bashell is havin' a hard time with his gunmen. They're located out there t' hell an' gone, and time's heavy on them. Thet type likes to hang aroun' saloons an' easy women—an' thet damn' desert doesn't have a one of them things."

Will Cooper rubbed his hands together to remove well-dirt. "You got a good strong point there, Apache. Fact is, I'm gettin' damn' tired of this waitin' game, too—but I don't want no boys killed. I'll wait, even if it means mebbeso the death of a thousan' or so head of Hatchet cattle."

Apache Ike gazed thoughtfully out the haymow's south window. Through it, he could see Hatchet's ranch-house. Anna Cooper had already lit a kerosene lamp. Apache Ike guessed at the woman's loneliness.

"An' another reason, Apache?"

"This trouble cain't go on forever. It isn't only Hatchet an' Bashell an' thet Arnaiz gundog, an' them homesteadin' gunmen. There's the people of Gila City, too."

Will solemnly nodded.

"They're bein' caught in the middle. Two men have been shot in their town, the last few days. One was killed, the other I jus' wounded. But I'd not be su'prised to learn that if they haven't sent word to Emil Dickinson, to hightail down here in a hell of a hurry, they're seriously thinkin' of such a plan. Nobody's safe on the street."

Will nodded agreement. When Apache Ike and Frank Hoffard had gunfought it out on Gila City's main street—and only street—a group of town's children had been playing marbles in the street.

"They'd fled for safety, bullets cutting the Arizona heat.

Will said, "I'll get Jennie to call a meetin' in the town hall tomorrow, *siesta* time."

The town hall was the saloon. Apache Ike said, "You got her in the saloon when her pappy was buried, but I doubt if she'll enter it again for such a thing as a town-meetin'. I got a hunch that little redhead don't cotton to saloons. You hook up with her an' your saloon-days are over, son."

Will smiled. "That won't break my heart. But I ain't asked her yet. An' if you ain't been asked, you cain't say *ro* or *yes*."

What'd you aim to do?"

"About Jennie?" Will said, jokingly.

"Yeah, about Jennie," Apache Ike said almost cynically.

Will laughed. "Don't let your distrust of women show, Apache. All of them ain't like Anna Cooper, I'm happy to say.

"We'll blast out that granite about tomorrow afternoon 'cause the hole'll be deep enough then. I still don't see how all these years I never learned about Abe diggin' them deep wells, an' gettin' only gypsum. Seems to me like I'd have been bound to hear about it from somebody in all that time."

"Things like that happen, I guess."

"Well, that's a bygone. Water so far in thet granite is bitter. Not even a cow dyin' of thirst would drink it."

"How about these cattle them gunmen is collectin'?"

"I'll lay that in your lap, Apache. You keep track of 'em, eh?"

"Okay. Got guards out for the night?"

Will had. Will left for his bunk. Apache Ike undressed to his skin and sat naked where the breeze between the haymow doors would strike him. From where he sat on a sack of oats, he saw the ranch-house.

He was still sitting there when he saw Anna Cooper's lamp go out.

Moonlight moved in and held the desert. He heard the distant lowing of water-starved cattle. The sound would be coming from Strawberry Springs, he figured—for the wind blew from that direction. And he'd long ago learned that sound carried far and easy in the clean desert breeze.

He slept sitting on the oats sack. He was awake at dawn when Hatchet began to stir. Guards came in and hit their bunks and new guards went out, two of them— on to patrol the southern half-circle, the other the northern half-circle.

Hatchet breakfasted and went to work.

Will glanced at his mother as he, his crew, wagon and team noisily passed the house. His mother's back was toward him. She did not turn. She kept on doling out water to her plants.

Will looked ahead.

He did not ride ahead of his crew this morning. The dynamite was safely buried down-coulee, two hundred yards. He'd left two hands at the diggings as guards.

They reported nothing but time had passed their way. One had slept the forepart of the night; the other, the latter part.

Beta's father and brother again were hired by the day. Jennie swung old Maude off-trail, Beta riding the side-saddle behind the redhead.

Will had loaned Jennie the side-saddle when he'd loaned her Maude. For some reason, there were three side-saddles on Hatchet. His father had bought them before he'd been born, Apache Ike had related.

Anna Cooper had not liked the first saddle her husband had bought. He'd then bought another, but that did not please his wife, either—so he had bought the third, which received the same lack of praise from his wife.

Abe Cooper had given up in despair on side-saddles. Apache Ike had reported the cowman had wanted his wife to sometimes ride range with him, something Anna Cooper never did.

A flat-brimmed black sombrero graced Jennie's wealth of red hair. Her white blouse rustled in the breeze. She had a new buckskin riding-skirt and new boots.

She'd bought these on time at the merc. Each resident of Gila City had a certain amount of credit at the

169

Cooper stores and she'd apparently used hers.

Beta was a little Spanish queen—dark of the eye, her white teeth glimmering as she smiled, which was most of the time.

Beta was now Jennie's assistant. She sorted out sales-slips according to dates, while Jennie made totals. She received fifty cents a day.

Jennie said to Will, "I've made up my mind, Will."

"Will looked at her. "You finally goin' to say yes to marryin' me, eh?" He grinned, but the grin was forced.

Jennie smiled. "No, not that. I'm postponing that, hoping a more handsome man comes along."

"I thank you," Will said.

Jennie said, seriously, "When are you going to blast?"

"This afternoon, unless some snag comes along. Why did you ask?"

"Well, if you hit sour water—and not sweet—I'm cutting that fence, Bashell or no Bashell."

Will shook his head. "No, you don't, Miss Clark. I don't want Bashell mad at you. I think the man's a maniac. If not all *loco*, part *loco*. It's take a demented brain to think of the plan he's usin' to get hol' of Hatchet. An' I don't want your life on Hatchet's conscience."

"You mean—he might kill me?"

"He sure might," Will said. "Don't underestimate the man's evilness one bit, Jennie."

"Will's right," Beta said.

Jennie said, "Come hell or high water, as my father used to say—if you don't hit sweet water, I'll cut that fence. And I've got the fence pliers to cut it. Dad and I built it and I can take it down.

"I'll find your wire-cutters an' hide them," Will said.

She laughed shortly. "I got them hid where nobody

can find them. Get along, Maude."

Will watched the girls ride into the brush and out of sight. He then busied himself, helping his crew get the well-casing down into the granite ledge. Apache Ike reported in at noon.

He got Will to one side. "I didn't climb to the top of Signal. I only went half-ways up, but that was high enough."

"What'd you see?"

"Arnaiz an' Bashell. They left town, ridin' south."

Will frowned. "Gassman Coulee is northwest of town, not south."

"That's so, but they rode south. About five miles out of town, they circled west, then got beyond Smoke Tree Arroyo. Then they turned their broncs north."

Will nodded knowingly. "Threw off any trailers or suspicion by riding south. Then when clear of town— an' the eyes there—they turned west, an' now are in Gassman, eh?"

"That's the deal."

"What're you goin' a do now?" Will wanted to know.

"I'll keep an eye on the herd. I know them cattle. All longhorns, not a bit of Hereford or Angus blood in 'em; an' they'll be ringy as a turpentined *coyotie,* Will."

"That they will. There's hardly any water in Gassman. I was over there about a week ago. Jus' a little out of the granite. Hell, by now that might be all dried up, for all I know."

"They smell this Strawberry water an' they'll go plumb mad, Will. Lower their horns an' charge, an' no barbwire fence this side of hell can stop 'em—if one in the hot place even could, which I doubt."

Will smiled. "I don't figure the ol' devil as a fence-maker," he said.

"You got your plans made?" Apache Ike said. "Got

the crew warned, an' all thet?"

"Thet I have," Will said.

Apache Ike nodded. "I see you durin' the ruckus, son." he neckreined his blue-roan gelding around and rode northeast, giving the impression he was heading back to Hatchet's home-*rancho*.

But he did not ride to the ranch. He crossed west of the spread and within an hour again crouched halfway up Signal Butte, field-glasses lying on a sandstone ledge to his right.

He closed his eyes, weariness sagging him—the weariness of age that a human never loses, once time forces it upon him. He was in the shade of a gray smoke-tree but the air was very hot.

He sat that way for some minutes with his aged eyes closed, and with memories moving in and playing their part, then disappearing as mysteriously and completely as before they visited.

He opened his eyes.

He reaced for his field-glasses. He trained them west on Gassman. To make clear seeing he has to refocus them. His gnarled fingers slowly turned the knurled knob, while he wondered idly why field-glasses always had to be refocused.

Bashell and Arnaiz were far to the west. They were a quarter-mile apart, Bashell to the north, Amaiz to the south, hazing Hatchet cattle out of the *malpais* and *chaparral*.

Not many Hatchet cattle were in the brush. Most were gathered around fenced-in water-holes. Nevertheless, the pair found steers and cows and hazed them toward Gassman, to the east.

The pair knew how to haze cattle out of the brush and rough country. Had he not known they had been in that area he undoubtedly would not have seen them, for they rode the canyons, coulees and the highest part of the brush. They knew how to keep hidden.

That stood for their gunmen-homesteaders, also. Apache Ike felt grudging admiration. These men were tough and they knew their nefarious trade. They kept the herd hidden in Gassman.

All they'd have to do—when the right time came—was to drive the stock out of the mouth of Gassman, going south; then they'd wheel them and move along a coulee, and then come out of this a quarter mile north of Strawberry Springs—where Will and Hatchet's crew was feverishly working.

From where he hunkered, he could not see down into Gassman. He lacked altitude. Therefore, he slowly and soberly climbed the old Apache trail down which he had come yesterday.

He had to climb to the very top of the Butte, before he had height enough to see the complete herd. He was surprised at the size of the herd. His practiced eye told him at least four thousand head were in the bunch.

They were milling and pawing in the wide coulee's bottom. Bulls threw up sand as they pawed. Calves frolicked for calves drank little water and therefore, the barbwire fences meant nothing to them.

Their mother's udders fed them. Although those udders undoubtedly held less milk because the cows had little if any water, they held enough to give their calves jump and bounce.

The calves were the only really active bovines. Bulls mounted cows in heat, for on this range a calf could come any time of the year—no snow or blizzard froze him to death if he were an early-spring calf.

His memory slipped back to the days when he and Abe Cooper had been young and strong and full of hell, back on the *Llaros Estacaos*—the Staked Plains—of the old Lone Star State, good old Texas.

He remembered rounding-up Hatchet cows to trail-drive into the Indian-infested high grass desert of Arizona Territory. All steers had been sold. Only a few bulls and six thousand head of cows made the trip. Even the calves had gone under the butcher's knife, for a calf was just a nuisance on such a long trek. And besides, he'd undoubtedly die on the trip, completely played out.

A total loss was a steer or a calf, on a trail drive.

Back on the Texas plains, a cow took a bull in July or June but no earlier; for this would have the cow throw the calf in April or late March. No danger of the calf freezing to death in a Texas blue-norther, one of those high Texas Panhandle winds that swept down from Colorado and the Rocky Mountains—a wind ice-cold and laden with snow and sleet.

Thus, the old Indian dozed and lived with his past, and therefore he did not look southeast at the Hatchet *hacienda*, for he had no reason to watch Hatchet—his job was to watch the rustlers and Bashell and Arnaiz.

The day moved on. The sun heeled over, still holding scorching heat. And because he did not look toward Hatchet he did not see the woman, dressed in black, leave the house by the back door and sneak into the barn where she saddled a horse and rode out side-saddle, disappearing into the brush.

The woman carried a rifle.

Chapter Fifteen

That day before leaving Gila City, Fred Bashell tied a gunny sack tightly across the back skirts of Mike Amaiz's saddle. You could see that the sack held a long cylinder.

"What's that?" Amaiz asked.

"Bologna," Bashell said.

Amaiz looked at his boss. "What the hell you sayin', anyway? Why pack along a round of sausage?"

"To eat, of course."

Amaiz reached back and felt, "Sure is hard," he said. "Must be old."

"But damn' good chewin'," Fred Bashell informed.

Amaiz asked, "Why didn't you tie it to your own kak? You ain't got nothin but your ol' yellow slicker tied there, an' why you pack a raincoat in this kentry is beyon' yours truly."

Fred Bashell swung into leather. "You ask a hell of a lot of questions." He smiled but his words had an undertone. "You ask more questions than that damn' fourth wife I had."

Arnaiz smiled. "Thought you was goin' say your fifth. How many times you been married, boss?"

"You mean married legally?"

"Yeah, legally."

Only onct. I was seventeen. She was a pro hooker, about twenty-one. All I guess she wanted of me was to pimp for her, an' I never was made for a street-corner hawker."

"Never again, legally?"

"You said it, Mike."

"Thet Jennie an' thet spic girl sure sidetracked us," Arnaiz said. "We sure was left holdin' the empty bag on the snipe hunt."

Bashell said, "You done with the salt cellar? If you are, pass it to me, huh?"

Arnaiz looked at his boss. "What'd you mean, boss?"

"I'll put some salt in your wound, too."

Mike Arnaiz showed white teeth in a laugh. "Let's hit the trail."

They rode south. Two hours later, they were deep in the brush pointing Hatchet stock into a herd. Suddenly, Fred Bashell disappeared. Mike Arnaiz wondered where his boss was gone, but made no inquiries of the other cowpunchers.

Fred Bashell had swung out on a scouting trip. He had heard in town that all cowpunching activities had been halted by Will Cooper's orders on Hatchet. Cooper evidently didn't want any of his cowpunchers blundering into trouble with any of the gunmen-homesteaders.

Will Cooper had been playing a waiting game, Fred Bashell knew. Cooper could afford to sacrifice a few thousand head of his longhorns. He ran about twenty thousand, they'd reported to Bashell in Gila City.

Also, they were longhorn stock. And longhorns had

little value on today's beef market. Housewives demanded more tender, succulent steaks. Longhorns didn't have much such steaks.

Longhorns were more bone, grizzle, hide and horns than Angus or Hereford or Shorthorns, or any of the bred-up beef strains. Also now that cattle were shipped to market instead of being trailed, you couldn't get many longhorns into a cattle-car because their horns made this impossible.

Some cowmen dehorned their longhorns before shipping. This weakened the steer, though; he lost lots of blood when he had his horns cut off. Others hired hands to wham each longhorn between the horns as he went up the loading-chute to the car.

Usually, the longhorn was hit with a heavy club. This loosened his horns at the roots. Two sidewise blows usually knocked his horns free. When dehorned in this manner, the base of the horns bled less than if sawed off or cut by dehorning shears.

Señora Gonzalez had said Hatchet was on the verge of shipping in registered Hereford bulls when the homesteaders had moved in and distracted Will Cooper's attention—and his roaring six-guns.

When a polled Hereford bull mounted a bony longhorn cow the offspring usually was without horns and a good rustler for this desert country, where it took at least twenty acres to feed a cow and calf.

Bashell had seen mixed breeds—longhorn, Hereford or Angus or Shorthorn—browse like deer, heads upraised as they stripped rich *mesquite* beans from their thorny vines.

Some cowmen were introducing the blood of Brahmas—the sacred cow of India—into their herds. A mixed-blood calf with Brahama was usually tan or sorrel, with a small hump. He could get fat where a longhorn or blooded calf starved to death.

He also was tick-free. The dreaded Texas fever—caused by tick bites—didn't effect him. Something in his skin disagreed with the tick's appetite, apparently—for the deadly ticks never rode a bovine with a bit of Brahma blood.

Bashell knew that the next boss of Hatchet—the eastern millionaire who wanted Hatchet—had great plans for the ranch. He'd get rid of all longhorns and run Hereford cows and Brahma bulls. Within a few years, he'd have a top mixed breed that would grow fat on water and *mesquite* beans.

Bashell dismounted on a high ridge, bronc hidden by smoke-trees, and he studied the rugged terrain below, eyes missing nothing. Below him, two desert lobo wolves loafed in the shade of a desert cottonwood. He saw something lying around that looked like the chewed-up remains of a Hatchet calf.

He wondered if the wolves had killed the calf, or had the calf died from lack of water for his mother? He decided on the former. Wolves liked fresh meat. They invariably killed their pray. Coyotes were the scavengers, Coyotes ate cattle already dead.

The reason for that was apparent. These two wolves—evidently a dog and his bitch—were almost as big as a small calf. He'd seen them kill calves.

They jumped the calf and caught him in a few strides. One went under—usually the bitch—and the dog went for the throat. Between the two of them, they sent the bawling calf rolling to his death.

A coyote couldn't kill a calf. The coyote was too small. His game was jackrabbits, mostly—and digging out kangaroo rats and mice. He and the wolf had one thing in common beside both being canines—the coyote and wolf invariably hunted in pairs.

One coyote would start the jackrabbit running. He had no chance of catching a big jack, for the jack had too much speed. So the coyote merely loped behind, the jack spurting ahead now and then.

The jack didn't notice, evidently, that the coyote was running him in a big circle. Each time he tried to dart to one side, there was the coyote heading him off.

When they passed the spot where the second coyote was hidden, the first coyote fell out to rest. The second took after the Jack, who of course couldn't tell one coyote from the other.

But the new coyote had a sudden burst of power that the jack figured he shouldn't have had, for the jack found himself tiring. Again, he was run in a big circle; again, a rested coyote took after him.

And the jack was getting tired. And the coyote, for some reason didn't seem to tire.

The resting coyote came in when the jackrabbit was exhausted. When fangs tore into the rabbit, he gave the only loud cry he would give in his entire life—a soul-rending scream of death.

And coyotes would feast, jowls red and bloody.

The sky was filled with buzzards. They circled on air currents, sometimes wafting high, then slowly swinging down. Suddenly, an entire flock of them would disappear below the horizon.

They had landed to gorge on some dead animal. They were the scavengers of the plains. Each animal—each bird—played his part here on the great American desert, and each was necessary.

Fred Bashell saw no danger in the area below. He could not see Strawberry Springs. It lay beyond a high rise to the southeast. He looked toward Hatchet. He could dimly make out the *rancho's* buildings in the far distance.

Would he be occupying that huge ranch by this time tomorrow? Would he be boss of Mussampa inside of a few hours? Or, would he be shot through and dead?

He grinned wolfishly. He was a sure believer in Fate. He thought a man's path was made out for him at birth. No matter what the man did to change the course of his life, he couldn't change it.

Fate made a man travel one route, and one only. Fate deemed he couldn't break from that route. If he were destined to win today, then win he would. If he were doomed to die today, then die he would.

It was that simple, that elemental.

A man died where and when Fate had so ordained. He went to his horse and continued his circle. He came in from the south and then he came silently out of the brush, Mike Amaiz twisted on stirrups, his .45 leaping from holster into his hand.

Amaiz angrily said, "God dammit it, Bashell, give a man some warnin'! I almost let this hammer drop!"

Fred Bashell laughed soundlessly. "Hell of a hand you are, Mike. Here I come up on horseback an' scare the bejabbers out of you, an' surely you must've heard my bronc in the bresh."

"I was chousin' out a ringy critter. I never had time or the chance, 'cause my bronc an' the critter was makin' noise brush-poppin'!"

Fred Bashell hid his smile. The closest cow he could see was a good hundred yards southeast, heading with her spring calf toward Gassman and the rest of the Hatchet herd.

"Where you bin?" Mike Amaiz asked. "I never seen you drop out."

Bashell told him of his exploratory circle. "Seems odd Cooper ain't got a han' or so out on scout; but if he has one or two I sure never seen 'em, an' I looked good."

"Ain't logical," Arnaiz said.

"What ain't logical?"

"Thet Cooper don't know we is gatherin' this herd. Hell, you cain't chouse critters on this desert without bein' seen, even if the one who saw you wasn't even lookin' for you."

"He knows," Bashell said.

"Then why ain't him an' his cowpokes doin' somethin' to stop us?"

"Mebbeso he don't want to stop us...right now?"

Mike Arnaiz studied him. "Come ag'in? I didn't catch you the first time aroun', Fred."

"He's got his plans," Fred Bashell said, "an' we got ours. When our plans clash, then we clash—an' the winner gets Mussampa."

"An' the loser?"

Again, that soundless laugh. "You kin guess at that, Mike." Sudden steel crept into Bashell's voice. "I don't know about you. Mebbeso your gun ain't as big as your mouth. You try to sagehen outa this an' if Hatchet don't kill you, Bashell does."

"Watch for yourself," Mike Arnaiz warned.

For a long moment, they studied each other. Sitting sweaty, hard-breathing horses, the only sound heard was the creak of saddle-leather. Their eyes were cold— they watched.

Both were ready. Nothing bound them but greed. There was no friendship, no camaraderie, between them. There never had been. There never would be. Only one element bound them together, and that was greed.

When each had attained his goal—when his greed had been satisfied—each would leave the other...if he were living. But now, each played a dangerous game, and each needed the other.

This need lifted their white-knuckled hands from the grips of their six-shooters. It forced each to smile a false smile.

Bashell quietly said, "We're gettin' ringy, Mike. This pressure—Well, soon it should be over, compadre. Mussampa should be ours. An' with Mussampa, we get Hatchet."

"Yeah," Mike Arnaiz cynically said. "We do the fightin'. We bleed if there's blood to be shed. We get killed, if there's killin'—an' there's bound to be. An some soft-handed rich bastard back east right now loafs with a tall glass of booze with ice in it—an' he takes over Hatchet, when we get done."

"He doesn't get Hatchet," Bashell said.

Mike Arnaiz asked, "How come you say that?"

"We keep Hatchet. There's a fortune to be made here. Breed up these longhorns, somehow get more water. This rich bug don't get Hatchet. You an' me do, friend. Understan'?"

"We steal Hatchet from this rich guy?"

Bashell grinned. "We don't steal it from him. He ain't never had it, nor never will. An' you cain't steal somethin' from some gink that he doesn't have."

"Let's not get into big words," Mike Arnaiz said. "What if this rich guy hires guns to take it away from us—or try to take it?"

"We'll be righ where Cooper is now."

Arnaiz grinned. "I like that idea. I'd like ownin' a ranch. There's a lot of big-fronted Mexican girls in Gila City, too."

That's no lie," Fred Bashell said. "Well, let's punch *our* cows, amigo"

They swung into riding. The afternoon fell back and the sun sank behind the scarp far-west mountains, but still the cloyish desert heat persisted, hanging to the soil and dropping the dessert trees.

"Enough," Fred Bashell finally said. "We cut the herd down the middle, now."

His gunmen crowded around, loafing in saddles, horses breathing hard and covered with sweat.

Mike Arnaiz said, "Cut the herd? I don't foller you, boss."

Bashell waved a hand. "Take half the cows up that draw. Swing 'em over east of Strawberry. Stampede them down that canyon, directly onto the springs."

"An' the other half?" a gunman asked.

"They come in hell-for-leather from the north. That way, we'll have Hatchet penned on the east an' the south. I got a hunch Cooper won't look for us to hit from the east."

"Good idea," another gunman said.

"You know anythin' about dynamite?" Bashell asked the crew. "Any of you ever worked with black powder?"

"I have," a gunman said. "Powder monkey a few months, up in a copper mine in Colorady. Why ask, boss?"

Fred Bashell swung down. He went to Mike Arnaiz's horse and untied the sack. He took out a long tin cylinder. He took the cap off it and two sticks of dynamite, complete with fuses, slipped out—long and red-colored and deadly.

He handed one to the ex-powder monkey. "Throw this behin' the herd—or into it—at the right minute, Warden."

"I'll do that," Jim Warden said.

Mike Arnaiz stared at the dynamite. "No wonder you tied that to my kak," he said. "If it'd blowed up, I'd gone skatin' fast into hell."

Fred Bashell smiled.

"An' you tol' me it was bologna," Arnaiz said.

Chapter Sixteen

Apache Ike said, "They got a big herd—aroun' five thousan' head—gathered. Unless I'm a cross-eyed pack-rat, they're due to hit this evenin'."

Will Cooper said, "We're ready."

"They'll come out of the big draw there." Apache Ike pointed north.

"Everythin' ready for the bastards," Will Cooper said. "We'll jus' pretend to be workin', but when the herd comes we'll all be on horseback. Which is the best for this range of fightin'? A rifle or a six-gun?"

Apache Ike grinned. "Both," he said. He looked at the well-casing. Only a few feet of it protruded above the muddy, alkali-laden water. "Punched it really down," he said.

"Down dèep," Will said.

"What kind of water come up the casin'?"

Will grimaced. "Soda an' then some. Sour as all billy-hell."

"How about the dynamite?"

"Jackson'll pop it the minute the herd comes down. That would scare them an' send 'em runnin' the other way. I sure hope we've guessed right. If we ain't, what other openin' do they have?"

"None I kin think of, son."

Hank Jackson worked around the casing. He was mud to the shoulders and sopping wet. "She's set to blow, boss."

"Got plenty of fuse?"

"Enough, I figure."

The rest of the crew busied themselves on imagined jobs. The men were tense and tight underneath. This showed in their jerky movements, their slightly paled faces, their guns tied down, their rifles leaning against scrub-trees close at hand.

Hatchet saddle-horses were in the brush to the south. They stood with reins dragging, cinches tight, rifles in saddle-boots, stocks sticking up ready for instant pulling.

All a puncher had to do was run across a fifteen-foot clearing, tear into the buckbrush, vault into saddle and pull his rifle as he rose—and he was ready for business, mounted on a fast horse and armed.

Apache Ike said suddenly, "Good lord, son, look who's comin'!"

Will Cooper, muddy, wet clothes, whirled, looked toward Gila City. Old Maude was a quarter-mile away, with Jennie holding the reins and Beta riding behind Jennie's side-saddle.

Will's heart fell.

"We gotta get 'em outa here," he said. "I got work here—or at least, pretend to work. Head 'em off, eh?"

"If I can, Will."

Apache Ike hurried to meet the women. And, at that moment, all hell broke loose. Stampeding cattle, longhorned, ugly, ready to fight anything on foot or horse-back, poured out of the coulee two hundred yards north. A mighty roar sending cows and calves and steers flying upward.

"Dynamite!" Will roared. "Explode it, Jackson!"

Hatchet men sprinted for horses. Will waited until Jackson had the fuse burning, then he took it on the run for his horse, Hank Jackson on his heels. They hit saddles, whirled, loped madly east—and then, to Will's surprise, cattle poured, mad and crazy, from the coulee directly ahead of them. They were bearing down madly on Hatchet—with Jennie and Beta and Apache Ike caught between Hatchet and the stampeding cattle.

Again, another roar in a herd of cattle.

Cattle soared upward, dust rising under them. Will glimpsed hunches and intestines and hides and heads floating upward, as though in a bad dream. One steer, intact, bawling, rose higher than the others, hesitated, then plummeted down, disappearing in the dust.

A cow's head hit Will in the right shoulder. It almost knocked him down. With sickening force, he realized he had erred in his battle-plan. He'd not counted on a herd stampeding in from the east.

Apache Ike had not reported Bashell cutting the herd in two. Had Bashell split the herd when the old man had last reported in, surely Apache Ike would have told him this.

His battle-plan had been to head east on thundering hoofs, and get behind the gunmen-homesteaders. Now, cattle bearing down from the east threw that plan into instant discard.

He had to get the women out of this. Already Jennie had wheeled old Maude, Beta screaming and hanging onto the side-saddle's hind strings. Old Maude was no fool.

186

Ears back, the wise mule pounded to the south, and never before had Will seen a mule run so fast. Jennie hung onto the saddle's fork, and Beta hung onto the saddle-strings as the old mule lurched, shod hoofs tearing Arizona soil in her speed.

Will rode close and hollered, "Hang on, women!" His short-gun was in his grip, and he twisted in leather.

Then, the fuse burned down—and the charge in the well-casing exploded. Just then, the lead steers of the northern stampede hit the well-area. Again, beef flew upward, some in whole carcasses; other in hunks of raw, bleeding, bovine flesh.

The explosion was stronger and more deadly than the other two. The well-casing shot upward, split from end to end. It soared higher than the highest hunk of beef.

Will saw the well-casing hit a flying cow. He saw water spout out of the well. The stream shot upward, some ten feet or so. A cow ran into the stream, slipped, fell.

Old Maude made it to the edge of the herd. A polled bull hit her on the rump. She slid, skidded, almost fell—her two riders hanging on desperately.

Then the mule was on safe ground, the cattle thundering past. Will's horse leaped desperately, ears back. He scrambled to safety, the herd whipping past his flowing tail.

"Get up on the hill," Will shouted to the women. "Look at 'em hit your spring-wagon, Jennie!"

A bull lifted the spring-wagon with his horns. Two cows thudded into it, overturning it. It disappeared under tons of mad beef.

Will neckreined his bronc, looking north into the sea of bovine backs. Old Apache Ike had been caught. His bronc was down, but the old Indian and two Hatchet hands were taking care of themselves, out there in those tons of rolling beef.

Their six-shooters spouted smoke. Their only hope was to pile up in front of them a high barrier of dead cows. This they were doing. Even as Will sent a glance that way, a cow leaped over the dead ones in front of the Hatchet men.

Apache Ike ducked. The cow roared overhead. She landed in a heap, other beeves pounding her flat.

"Kill Cooper! Five hundred bucks to the man who kills Will Cooper!"

The cry came from across the herd. Through the dust and the darkening night, Will barely made out the gunmen-homesteaders. The gunmen were spreading out, riding hard along the rim of the cattle.

Will spurred forward, six-gun in hand. His horse staggered, almost fell; he then noticed the fork of his saddle was split. He understood. A bullet had torn into the saddle, the force almost dumping his lunging mount.

Rifles snarled. Six-shooters roared. Horses neighed. reared, fought bits and spurs. Dust rose in choking clouds.

Will glimpsed Hank Jackson and a Bashell gunman fighting hand to hand, knives upraised. Jackson saw an opening.

He buried his Bowie to the hilt in his adversary's throat. The gunman staggered back. He disappeared in the stampeding cattle.

Then Will saw Bashell.

A hundred feet north, Bashell fought a rearing, striking horse, Winchester held high, as he peered into the dust,there on the east rim of the stampeding Hatchet cattle.

Will's .45 came up. He cried, "Bashell over here! Will Cooper!"

Bashell saw him, then. His rifle came down. Will's .45 was on the land-locator. Both were ready to shoot.

But neither shot.

For a woman rode out of the brush. She was dressed in black and she rode a black horse with a black leather side-saddle. She carried a rifle. She said, "Bashell!"

Bashell stared, Will Cooper momentarily forgotten. Will also stared. He couldn't believe his eyes.

Dust rose in a cloud, giving Anna Cooper a ghoulish appearance. Her black horse stood stock-still, despite the running cattle two hundred feet west. Her rifle was at her shoulder, barrel centered on Bashell.

She screamed, "Men of War Axe, we have come! The devil is ahead. We have him under our rifle's sights, riders of Bad Axe!"

Her eyes glistened with fanatical light. Evidently she imagined she had guns and riders behind her? And *War Axe?* And *Bad Axe?* She had even forgotten the name Hatchet?

"Kill, men of Axe Handle," she screamed.

And her rifle spat lead.

Horror-stricken, Will Cooper stared, frozen to his saddle.

Bashell shot first.

Bashell shot three rapid, roaring shots. Will saw his mother's thin body flinch. The bullets almost dehorsed her.

Nevertheless, she shot two times.

Her first bullet missed. Her second caught Fred Bashell under the chin. It almost decapitated him. He went over backwards in his saddle. His horse reared, whirled, and ran toward the herd, then skidded to a stop—and Bashell sailed on into the stampeding cattle.

He landed on the back of a bony longhorn cow. She bucked him off. He disappeared then, falling into the slashing hoofs.

Will hurriedly dismounted. He ran to his mother, there on the ground; her black was running toward the eastern hills, head to one side so he'd not step on his trailing reins.

Will noticed that Jennie had left old Maude. Jennie was catching Anna Cooper's bronc, grabbing for the reins.

Heart hammering, he knelt beside his mother. One glance told him she was dead. Bashell's bullet had hammered over her heart.

Blood covered her black bodice.

Will picked her up. He carried her east to make sure the cattle wouldn't stampede after her. The herd had almost passed. Jennie came, leading Anna Cooper's horse.

Beta sat on the mule behind them.

Jennie said, "They're breaking. They're starting to run, Will."

Will only nodded. His throat was too dry, too constricted, for words. He saw old Apache Ike, across the dust, raise his rifle; for Mike Arnaiz faced the old *segundo*.

Both were on foot. Arnaiz also had a Winchester. He shot at Apache Ike. He shot too rapidly. He didn't take aim. Apache Ike did.

Apache Ike's bullet sent Arnaiz reeling. Arnaiz dropped his rifle. He turned as though to run. He even took a few steps. then, his knees went out and he landed on his face.

Apache Ike saw Will. He raised his rifle and waved it. Will heard a Bashell gunman holler, "Bashell—He's down, men, down!"

Another hollered, "Arnaiz is down, too."

"Get outa here," another said.

They ran for their horses. They hit saddles. Those already mounted were already riding madly away, heading for the thick western chaparral.

Will yelled, "Let 'em go, men."

Within seconds, chaparral hid the gunmen. The last of the cattle ran past. Holding his dead mother in his arms, Will Cooper stood there and looked around, red-headed Jennie Clark beside him.

Cattle had completely taken out the clark fence surrounding Strawberry Springs. Barbwire lay in lengths. Only one post remained upright.

The Clark spring-wagon lay on its side, one wheel lazily spinning. The team was nowhere in sight.

"Your horses," Will said. "They must've run off ahead of the stampede."

Jennie said, "They're in the dug-out. I saw them run in there."

Apache Ike walked slowly toward them. He looked at dead Anna Cooper and said, "I didn't understan' her in life, Will. An' I guess I sure couldn't understan' her in death." His head was bare, his hat lost in the strife. "But if ol' Abe'd been here, he'd say she died a brave person, an' I guess that's what really counts."

Standing wide-legged, still holding his mother's bloody body, young Will Cooper looked about, seeing the hoof-mangled form of dead Hank Jackson beside that of he man he'd killed, Jim Warden.

Cattle were drinking at Strawberry Springs.

"I'll straighten the spring-wagon," Apache Ike said. "I'll harness the team. I saw them run into the dug-out."

He hurried away. Will saw the boy shimmy down from a cottonwood tree. He walked to the well Hatchet had blasted. The earth had caved in around it. The effort had been useless.

But now, Hatchet would have water. Without Bashell to pay their wages, the gunmen-homesteaders would abandon their homesteads, thus relinquishing their homestead rights—and throwing the land open again for homesteading.

Hatchet punchers would now file homesteads on the springs. He'd then buy their homestead rights, when they got their deeds from Uncle Sam.

Apache Ike hollered, "The spring-wagon's ready, son."

Will carried Anna Cooper to the spring-wagon. He remembered the first time he'd seen this rig and Jennie. Jennie had picked a tub of chokeberries. Now, Jennie laid a blanket on the rig's bed.

Gently, Will put his dead mother on the blanket. Jennie's hand caught his. She said, "Will, do you want me with you?"

Will Cooper looked into her blue eyes. "Yes," he said and added, "Hatchet needs you, Jennie."

"Thank God for that," Jennie said.